AGUA

EDUARDO BERTI

AGUA

Translated from the Spanish
by Alexander Cameron
and Paul Buck

with an Afterword by
Alberto Manguel

PUSHKIN PRESS
LONDON

© Eduardo Berti, 1997
Afterword © Alberto Manguel, 2001

First published in Spanish
by Tusquets Editores, Barcelona, 1998

English translation © Alexander Cameron
and Paul Buck 2003

This edition first published in 2003 by
Pushkin Press
123 Biddulph Mansions
Elgin Avenue
London W9 1HU

British Library Cataloguing in Publication Data:
A catalogue record for this book is available
from the British Library

ISBN 1 901285 42 1

Frontispiece: © Laura Lavergne

Set in 10 on 12 Baskerville
Designed by Blacker Limited
and printed in Britain by
Henry Ling Limited at the Dorset Press, Dorchester

AGUA

A journey in space
equals a journey in time.

WALLACE STEVENS
Adagia

It was in 1915
the old world ended.

D H LAWRENCE
Kangaroo

CHAPTER ONE

SINCE 1913, Luís Agua's life had consisted of visiting remote places in the central region of Portugal, offering his services as "the authorized representative of Douglas & Banks, the Energy and Lighting Company," as proclaimed on the business card he presented at each village.

A spark. A crackle. A light illuminated. Applause from the assembled. End of demonstration and Agua stepped forward.

"E-lec-tri-ci-ty!" he exclaimed, pointing at the lamp's flickering light.

Some could not believe their eyes and voiced their suspicions. Others could not understand how a lamp could light up without some means of fire. Each village reacted in the same way, with slight variations. People gathered around Agua and applauded him, as if he were a magician or entertainer. Only a few approached him with real interest, and they were always the most powerful.

Luís Agua praised the merits of his company by showing that all the equipment for his demonstrations could be fitted into just one suitcase. He explained how it was possible to use different sources of energy to obtain light, and if he did not have access to a petrol-powered motor, he would make do with a windmill or even improvise a dynamo with an old bicycle.

And then he would work the lever and after some humming sounds the bulb would illuminate. "E-lec-tri-ci-ty!" he would once more exclaim. And so, stepping forward, the villagers showered him with applause. He often dreamt of that moment.

The Portuguese State had supplied the firm of Douglas & Banks with a list of almost a hundred locations needing electricity. The list, however, was not exhaustive and the villages the company visited using its own initiative often yielded greater profits, since the State was not involved in the transactions.

Once a deal was struck, Agua departed, leaving the work of the installation of cables, electricity switches and lamps in the hands of the technicians. Every so often he returned to oversee the work and give his seal of approval to the operations in progress. As the majority of the villages still without electricity were located in the central region of the country, Luís Agua tired of travelling back and forth from his home in Lisbon. In order to shorten the length of his journeys, a month earlier he had chosen Coimbra as his place of residence.

In Coimbra, a university city, the sons of the wealthiest families in the land frequented the classrooms. Taking advantage of the fierce demand, the locals asked such high rents for the rooms that Agua reluctantly lodged in a boarding-house on Oliveira Matos, a street in the lower part of town. He was thinking of returning to Lisbon when someone told him of a small village called Vila Natal, the mention of which brought a poem to mind:

> *Living in a peaceful village*
> *From whence the road leads long and true*
> *Towards a place of blood and tears*
> *We are pure.*

If only, imagined Luís Agua, if only purity could be found so easily, with a simple geographical shift. Earlier generations had lived in pursuit of virgin paradises, but that era had disappeared with the heralding of modern times. Agua expected Vila Natal to offer the same vices that were characteristic of the big cities, though on a smaller scale. Despite the poem, it was not the adventure and still less the purity that he sought in the village, but its practicality. For the purpose of his business trips, Vila Natal was perfectly situated, and the lodgings modest.

He glanced down the list of villages the company had sent him: Vila Natal was not there. He sent a letter suggesting it be included, in case it was already on the list of Salvador da Silva, the other representative, but the reply from the director of the firm was laconic: "We have no mention of any village by the name of Vila Natal. We suspect it does not exist." As that response forbad nothing, three days later Agua cancelled several other appointments to pay a lightning visit to Vila Natal.

Lost in time, dominated by an impregnable castle, Vila Natal seemed, in the spring of 1920, like a village immune to the changes already a reality elsewhere. Only horse-drawn carts were seen on their roads. Candles were their only lighting. If some invisible giant was puffing the winds of progress, his breath was most definitely blowing in the opposite direction to Vila Natal. This did not bother the villagers for the simple reason they had never ventured outside the region and did not know just how much they were missing.

The night Agua arrived in the village, the place was deserted, shrouded by fog and an excessive stillness. Where were the people? The only sound to be heard came from a neighbouring belfry. In the church, a stout priest rang the bells, at the same time arguing with two of his altar boys.

"Didn't I tell you to watch the clock? You ring the bells at any time but the right one," the priest complained.

His tone was severe. The inefficiency of his helpers upset him to such an extent he had become distracted and, according to Agua's count, had already sounded the bells ten or twelve times when it was only nine o'clock.

"Where is everybody?" asked Agua, after introducing himself to the priest, who in turn introduced himself as Friar Teresino.

"Where are they?" repeated the Friar, glancing at the young altar boys.

"At the auction in the castle," replied one without giving further details.

Agua descended the church steps and returned to the road along which he had been venturing minutes earlier. A clattering of hooves drew his attention. Through the mist he thought he discerned two carriages.

"Halt! Are you heading for the castle?" he shouted, noticing the horses were harnessed.

Two carriages drove along the main street, but only the second slowed to allow Agua to climb in. There were five people inside: an elderly man, two middle-aged men and a kind-looking woman seated beside someone who appeared to be her daughter.

"Aha, I see we are many seeking the same treasure," said one of the men as Agua stepped aboard.

"It's not every day such events take place," said the woman.

"That's true," replied another of the men.

Agua bowed to the passengers and took his seat. The carriage swayed gently, enough of a sign for the coachman to spur on the horses.

"Has anyone read a description of the lots?"

It was the old man speaking. He ran a handkerchief over his forehead to mop up his sweat. His shrill voice showed signs of trepidation.

"I only ask because I was told there may possibly be an original Rembrandt. I find it hard to believe, I'm more inclined to imagine we'll come across a first-rate copy. There are copies with quality that have some worth ... but an original! Good Lord, it'd be worth more than we could afford between us all."

"Are you an art specialist or something like that?" asked the woman.

The old man, who called himself Mister Roger, replied that he was "something like that," adding that for many years he had visited Portuguese castles in search of valuable pieces, antiques and works of art.

"Economic hardship is hitting well-to-do families in the region," explained Mister Roger. "It's like a plague, misery. In its wake, the nobility find there's no alternative but to sell the treasures they've looked after for centuries."

This was apparently the case with Antunes Coelho's widow, whose castle the two carriages were heading towards. It was common knowledge in the village that, even though the woman lived in surroundings of luxury, nothing belonged to her except for two paintings inherited from her father. While waiting to resolve certain inheritance problems, the widow's only income derived from the land around the castle. To make matters worse, a terrible drought, the consequence of an abnormal heat wave, had ruined the last crop. In order to pay her debts, the lady had no choice but to sell her paintings. The auction succeeded not only in lifting the village out of its routine, it also brought together people from neighbouring places. Although many were interested in the paintings, many more came to assist, their sole aim to see the castle from within, its doors having previously been firmly shut to outsiders.

Those who had the leisure that night to see around the castle would have concurred in describing it as majestic: vast Persian carpets stretched from wall to wall and, outside, the black stone walls were overgrown with a thin shadow of moss. Situated on the outskirts of Vila Natal, a few hours by horse from the city of Coimbra, the magnificent edifice had been erected in the fifteenth century for the Antunes Coelho family, one of the oldest and most powerful in the region. In 1920, before its subsequent deterioration, its presence was still synonymous with opulence.

It took the carriage less than half an hour to reach the castle along the dirt track that joined Vila Natal to the river Barroso, a tributary of the Mondego. On arrival, Agua noticed seven other carriages had made it before them. Suddenly he felt somewhat ridiculous attending an auction with a suitcase. He waited for the others to descend from the carriage, slid his case under the seat and, taking the coachman aside, asked him not to leave without warning.

The whole village, it seemed, was gathered in the large park encircling the castle. Tall, her hair in a chignon to emphasize her upright demeanour, Fernanda Antunes Coelho was waiting for her visitors at the foot of a marble staircase. With tempered steps, Agua came forward to kiss her hand. He had to admit she looked splendid, just right for the occasion. She was around fifty, despite appearing ten years younger. Her haughtiness was barely concealed beneath her practiced gestures of goodwill.

"I've travelled the country, through many regions, but I've rarely seen a castle like this," Agua told her. And he was not lying.

The widow thanked him with a wry smile, her eyes sparkling briefly like emeralds. The following moment, Mister Roger accompanied by a gentleman with greyish hair ushered Luís Agua inside, into a room where the figure of a young man named Pedro Broyz stood out.

On seeing the Englishman enter, Broyz, who was mingling distractedly among the gathering, smoking an exquisitely aromatic Havana cigar, stepped forward to greet him. Agua noticed he was wearing a forced smile. There wasn't a great deal of warmth between them, even though Mister Roger had been the friend and administrator of his father some years earlier, in Broyz's youth.

As the auction was running late, Agua asked Broyz what profession he practiced, a simple question to pass the time. "I'm a doctor, but I'm not practicing. You see, medicine was never my true vocation," replied Broyz. The only other doctor in his family, he added, was a great grandfather—whose surname was not Broyz, but Schillman, Schulman, or something like that—who still enjoyed a certain amount of fame for having attended to Hegel in Berlin during the 1831 epidemic, the same outbreak that had forced Schopenhauer to flee to Frankfurt. Broyz hoped that such information about his ancestry would impress those present, but nobody made the slightest comment. Thus, after an awkward silence, he took his leave and went off in search of the widow.

"Gentlemen, please," announced the diminutive and stooped auctioneer. "Here we have two authentic masterpieces of world painting …"

People were congregating around the first painting, Manet's *Amazon Woman*. The auctioneer was already wielding his hammer when Mister Roger made his way unexpectedly towards the lower platform where the paintings were displayed and, with the help of his ivory cane, began a slow and careful inspection. Even though the auctioneer was glaring at him, this could not prevent Mister Roger from drawing the proceedings to a halt by announcing that the "genuine" Rembrandt and Manet on view were, in fact, mere copies.

"It's not possible. Are you sure?" exclaimed Broyz.

A murmur of disbelief rose from the assembled company. Nearly everybody awaited a sign from the auctioneer, who was looking at the widow, who in turn was looking at Broyz, who was himself looking at Mister Roger, who was looking at the auctioneer, along with nearly everyone else.

Reaching out with his stick, employing sweeping gestures,

the Englishman began to trace each line of the paintings, highlighting details that betrayed them as forgeries.

Fernanda immediately attempted to apologize to those in attendance. Other art specialists had never mentioned those details. Her father, originally, then later she and her deceased husband had believed the paintings to be authentic.

"Nobody doubts your good faith," Mister Roger hurried to reply, his expertise having captured the general admiration of those present, especially when he hazarded a guess at the name of the Rembrandt imitator.

Far from boasting, Mister Roger felt troubled for having discovered nothing but reproductions. Agua thought it his duty to console him. Everybody admired his knowledge and thanked him greatly for preventing an accidental swindle. Having said as much, Agua went over and took him by the arm as if he was his father. However, Mister Roger's true cause of restlessness was the antique chinaware on display in the glass cabinets and, still more, the bracelet of silver and rubies which danced on the widow's right wrist. The Englishman knew perfectly well that, according to the will, the widow was not authorized to sell the china, but was, on the other hand, authorized to sell either the bracelet or the paintings. Since nobody had even offered as much as a *centavo* for the reproductions, he thought now was the moment to strike a deal.

"Would you show me your bracelet, Senhora Fernanda?" he asked quietly, a moment later. "It's not my specialist field, you know better than I … but it's a wonderful piece of jewellery. Have you never thought of selling it?"

"The bracelet? I'm sorry, it's not for sale," apologized Fernanda amiably.

A look of disappointment crossed the old man's rugged face. He patted Luís Agua on the shoulder and together they left the place, and headed for the carriage waiting to take them back to Vila Natal. The coachman cracked his whip and the wheels rolled.

On the way, Mister Roger explained to Luís Agua that young Pedro Broyz was the widow's fiancé, no less. "He's twenty-five years younger than her," was his first comment, as if that worried him. "They met on the towpath along the riverbank, thanks to my introduction," he added with some pride. Realizing Agua was interested, he continued by telling him that a while back, one afternoon in October to be more precise, the widow had sent a messenger to summon him in order to seek financial advice.

"She's spent seven years shut away in that castle," said the Englishman. "Seven years since the death of her husband. She has spent the last of her savings, all the money inherited from Antunes Coelho, and though she survived thanks to the harvest, she was so badly advised that the land was still being ploughed with obsolete tools and machinery. She asked, 'What shall I do now?' I replied, 'Buy new machinery and consult a surveyor.' She said, 'With what money? I'm broke.' I said, 'In that case, get rid of the servants and sell the castle. With that money you can live in peace.' She laughed. 'What you suggest, that's impossible.' And it was only when she explained the reasons that I learnt about the will."

"What will? Put like that, it doesn't make sense ..." Agua protested.

"A moment," replied the Englishman. "In fact, her husband left a will, which I would describe as ... perverse. It was Antunes' wish that until she re-married, no part of the castle, or its possessions would belong to her: neither the furniture nor works of art, nor the gardens or stables. Incredible, isn't it?"

"Incredible. And so?" asked Agua.

"And so, as the will thwarted my suggestion she sell everything, I thought immediately of Broyz's father, a respectable business-man ... very dapper, despite being almost seventy. I don't think I told you, but the deceased husband was almost twice her age. When Antunes died, Fernanda was still a beautiful woman, and for a while a number of men from the village came to the castle with an eye for her and not the inheritance."

"Not the inheritance? That's hard to believe."

"Fernanda, in her semi-monastic seclusion, succeeded in keeping the will's conditions a secret. Do you follow?"

"I see."

"I said to Fernanda: 'You ought to marry a respectable and wealthy man like Ricardo Broyz.' As I saw it, Broyz was instrumental in removing the catch from the will. Furthermore, with his money and under my guidance as administrator, Fernanda could effectively cultivate those fields that had been so poorly exploited. 'Once married, you should mechanize the farm and establish better working methods,' I suggested. She listened to my ideas and finally agreed to meet Broyz, although she wasn't entirely convinced. Then it was my turn to persuade Ricardo. He'd been a widower for barely two years and was adamant that all women paled in comparison to the memory of his wife. Nevertheless, I persuaded him to accompany me to the castle one night. I introduced him to the lady and left them alone. They got on well together, as I found out the following morning. But not as well as I expected, and of the pair of them, it was he who seemed keener. After that, for two months, Fernanda turned down every invitation Ricardo Broyz proposed through me. Fed up with this role as matchmaker, I decided to lay a little trap for the widow, inviting her for a stroll along the riverbank without telling her that her admirer would be waiting there."

"A happy coincidence," joked Agua, laughing.

"Something like that. But don't think it was easy. There was nothing that lady hated more than to leave her castle. She had only done so on a few occasions, and always to visit the church in Vila Natal, or some nearby monastery, for example the one in Caminhos. Senhora Fernanda retains an extraordinary predilection for anything to do with religion and family ..."

"Stop!" interrupted Agua. "Please don't get side-tracked with details. I'm becoming impatient. What happened at that meeting?"

"What happened? Picture the scene. I'd taken up position a few metres from the boat cabin. I see the lady approaching. I wave my hand and she heads towards me smiling. We exchange a few words. People stare, surprised, unable to believe the widow has finally left her hide. Broyz is getting later and later, when suddenly a young man, whom I didn't recognize at first comes along."

"Let me guess. That fellow … was the son of Ricardo Broyz."

"Of course," replied Mister Roger.

"What did he want?"

"He was very anxious. He took me aside and started talking quickly, in a hush. 'Haven't you heard the news?' he asked. 'This morning, in the early hours, a fire destroyed my father's warehouse.' Of course I hadn't heard. Broyz's son then informed me that little or nothing had been saved from the flames, and that his father couldn't get over the catastrophe. 'Put yourself in my place,' he added. 'I arrived yesterday afternoon from Coimbra to find myself dealing with this state of affairs.' I tried to calm him. I asked why he hadn't contacted me earlier. I was supposedly the administrator of the business, as well as an old family friend. 'I've been looking for you ever since the fire broke out, Mister Roger, but my father was in such a shock he'd even forgotten you were supposed to be here.' Then I noticed Fernanda was following our conversation with great interest. 'Senhora Antunes Coelho,' I said, to say something, perhaps only to change the conversation, 'this young man is the son of Ricardo Broyz.' From that moment it was as if I'd become invisible. The young Broyz held out his hand. She expressed her condolences for the fire and, without a pause, he proposed they take a walk together along the river path. She couldn't refuse. It wasn't difficult to see the interest with which Pedro looked at the widow. At first, I thought Fernanda intended to take advantage of the son to ascertain more information about his father. How naïve of me! In reality she was choosing between the pair of them."

"But … what about the father?"

"Neither his son nor I talked to him about it. Nor was there any reason to. After three months the whole village was gossiping about the engagement between Pedro and the widow. Details of Antunes' will became common knowledge, everyone talking about the most constraining clauses, and everyone explaining the engagement in the light of those clauses. Ricardo's health deteriorated, gravely this time. His burial was a scandal. It was predictable: while the father had lost everything as a result of the fire, his only son was about to lay his hands on the greatest fortune in the region, assuming he married Fernanda. That's how it is, life's made up of lucky breaks. Of course, other people's good luck makes us envious, and many in Vila Natal, if not all, accused Broyz of being a bad son and a fortune hunter."

Luís Agua said nothing. He studied the Englishman's expression, trying to work out what his feelings were towards Broyz. Hadn't there been some slight tension before the auction, because the Englishman had also taken Broyz for a fortune hunter? Agua had no time to formulate that question. A third man, who was travelling with them in the carriage, and who, until that moment had remained silent, spoke up, offering the opinion that the young Broyz was only interested in Antunes' money, and that to achieve that end, killing his father was of little importance. Mister Roger vehemently leapt to the son's defence. Pedro Broyz, as he could testify, had fallen in love with Fernanda without any knowledge of her wealth or the inheritance.

"At times, certainly, he's unfriendly towards me, perhaps because he suspects I told his father about his engagement with Fernanda. But he's wrong … very wrong. Nobody cared for Ricardo's health like I did. He was my one true friend. I even paid for his last treatment out of my own pocket. Never mind, it's of no consequence. I respect Pedro Broyz because at that meeting on the banks of the river, he had just returned to the village after three years in Coimbra, and he knew nothing about Antunes or the relationship between his father and Fernanda."

The man murmured disapproval, which the Englishman ignored.

"And she?" said Agua, continuing with his questions.

"I don't think Fernanda is capable of loving Broyz. The age difference is an obstacle without doubt, but I believe she's incapable of forgetting her deceased husband. She's merely looking to gain possession through Broyz of the wealth of which the will deprives her."

There had been several days without rain in the village. The track was so dry the carriage wheels raised thick clouds of dust.

"In any case," continued the Englishman, "I understand Fernanda and Broyz will marry soon. Who would've thought …"

The horses slowed and the coachman announced:

"Vila Natal. We're here."

Luís Agua took out his case and descended first. After helping down the Englishman, he offered his hand, bidding him farewell.

"It's been a pleasure. I hope to see you on my return."

"What? Are you leaving?" asked Mister Roger. "You've just arrived and you're going already …"

"As a matter of fact, I'm leaving tomorrow afternoon," replied Agua, and he revealed his plans to settle in the village.

"Settle here? Wonderful! And where are you thinking of staying tonight?"

"I need you to recommend a boarding-house."

"A boarding-house!" exclaimed Mister Roger, and he began to laugh. "In this village, there is no place to stay … just like so many other things."

And so as not to disconcert Agua, the Englishman suggested:

"Please be my guest for the night."

Luís Agua could scarcely refuse, and off they went, on foot, to the Englishman's home.

"You'll love this village. Believe me, you've made the right choice deciding to settle here. And I think I can recommend some ideal lodgings: small, but in good condition. The only drawback, I'm afraid, is there are many precarious places and only a few really comfortable ones."

Agua replied that he would be content with renting a room.

"That's fine," said the Englishman. "For the same cost as a room in a boarding-house in Coimbra, you'll find lodgings here in a distinguished household. Why not in this very house, what do you say?"

Mister Roger was so talkative that it was only the next day, over lunch, that Luís Agua was able to speak about his work for the electricity company.

"How interesting!" exclaimed the Englishman. "Your arrival will be synonymous with progress."

"No need to go that far," said Agua, turning a darker shade of red. "What's more, I can't settle in quite yet. First, I must travel to other villages on business, then on my return, in about three to four months, I can rent a room somewhere."

CHAPTER TWO

BROYZ KNEW that Antunes Coelho's will stated: "to the new husband of my beloved, the greater part of my fortune." Yet Broyz did not understand how that man was capable of such a gesture without even knowing him. To his mind, it was madness. Or perhaps Antunes Coelho had supposed, before his death, that a woman as beautiful as his wife needed the help of an additional reward to find another husband.

It was only now that the matter of the reward filled Broyz with doubts. He felt unsure of his own feelings, his greed, about the comments of others. He felt under suspicion. It bothered him that so much money came between him and her. The late Antunes had sparked off a choir of suspicious voices from his tomb, thought Broyz. It was the perfect strategy to keep any suitor with a guilty conscience away from Fernanda. With a will of this sort, Antunes was setting a severe examination for the man who dared to succeed him. That brave person, no matter whom he was, would have to make his way to the altar repelling a mountain of rumours. Someone able to triumph over so much hearsay had to be, by nature, an irreproachable administrator. And if Antunes, like any man who laid down his life to build his fortune, had yearned for it to outlive him, the will existed precisely to prevent that money from being squandered, thought Broyz.

During his long morning walks with Fernanda, Broyz's main preoccupation was that the matter of the inheritance never came up, avoided by both with exaggerated circumspection. Broyz feared she might be offended if he mentioned the subject, feared she might sense the greed that he refused to acknowledge. But was he really greedy? He didn't know what to think about himself. It concerned him she appeared to forget the whole matter of the inheritance, as though it was an irrelevance. Perhaps she was also forcing herself to hide her interest in Antunes' money? Yet both knew, and said nothing precisely for that reason, that the wedding depended upon Fernanda being able to make use of the riches lying dormant in the castle. It was much like an arm wrestling match. Broyz could imagine two contestants, elbows on table, fingers interlinked: a struggle between the lady's pride and the husband's money; a struggle between the image Broyz wished to project in the village and the perverse reality imposed by the will.

Broyz did consider the alternative of marrying and at the same time renouncing the fortune. Secretly, he entertained this idea, and without a word to Fernanda, visited the notary of Vila Natal to seek permission to quietly examine the original text of the document.

"I'm afraid I can't help you. The will can only be consulted by the close family of the deceased," said the secretary and nephew of the notary. But Broyz bribed him with five banknotes and the youth led him through to his uncle's office. There he read:

"*I, the undersigned, João Paulo Pedro Jayme Antunes Coelho, sane both in body and mind, hereby express my final wish.*

"*Having no blood descendants, I bequeath all my savings to my wife Fernanda, without condition. As regards my possessions and belongings, in other words my castle and all that it contains, along with its adjoining lands, I also bequeath them to my wife Fernanda, on the condition that she remarries. Until such time, she may have no claim to my possessions, other than the profits from the agricultural lands. Only when she remarries, will she be able to lay claim to everything, although sharing the land and pos-sessions in unequal parts of one third and two thirds with her new husband. And of those parts, I bequeath to the new husband of my beloved, the greater part of my fortune.*"

Up to that point, the problem seemed resolved: he would refuse the money. It was simple enough to assign to Fernanda the two thirds Antunes intended to award him by making an inter vivos gift. However, further down the page, in an amendment to the document, a specific clause stipulated that the whole inheritance, including the third belonging to the widow, would be donated to a religious institution in the eventuality of Fernanda's new husband rejecting his share in favour of another person.

"Friar Teresino, who's the village representative for all charitable organizations, is aware of that clause," the notary pointed out, "and he won't miss the opportunity to invoke it if you marry the lady and, at the same time, renounce the inheritance."

Although Fernanda had always stood out among the benefactors who sustained the parishes of Vila Natal and Coimbra, Broyz didn't have the heart to do such a thing. How could he deprive her of the wealth to which she was entitled? What's more, Broyz viewed with contempt those charitable organizations, ever since the day he learnt that a director of an orphanage in Coimbra had enriched his personal wealth from donations received.

Before taking leave of the notary and his nephew, and profiting from a distraction on their part, Broyz managed to copy some paragraphs from the will into a small notebook. Over the following days, various villagers caught sight of him with the notebook under his arm strolling around the castle without seeking entry, or heading towards the river, away from prying eyes. The rumour had already swept through the village like wildfire; for everyone he was a crook chasing the inheritance without an iota of scruples. "What immorality," went the murmurs in Vila Natal.

And so it was that, notebook in hand and lost in thought, on the evening before his formal request for the widow's hand in marriage, Broyz arrived by chance outside the cemetery situated on the path to the river. He had never stepped through its dark gateway, not even after his father's death, something that had only increased the villagers' animosity towards him. There was nothing he hated more than to walk among tombstones, but this time something pushed him to enter. At the far end, amid the most spectacular vaults, stood the family mausoleum of Antunes Coelho. At the foot of a limestone promontory lay the tombs where the deceased were buried, where the lady herself would rest, and where, why not, thought Broyz, he too would end up, noble administrator of a family that had begun to fade from society for lack of descendants.

On the marble tombstone Broyz noticed a chain identical to

the bracelet. There it was, although without rubies, set right in its centre. He read the engraved:

"*João Paulo Pedro Jayme Antunes Coelho (1850-1911)*"

At the foot there was also the inscription:

"*The two of us for ever.*"

It was written in Latin beneath the round silver plaque. Broyz couldn't believe it. He'd made complimentary remarks about the bracelet without realizing that, by doing so, he'd praised their unshakeable union. Everything was now clear: Fernanda was chained to the memory of Antunes, and he would never be able to become a third part in that pact. By openly demonstrating his fondness for Fernanda, he had become the male instrument by which she would gain access to the inheritance.

It was getting dark. The shadows falling between the vaults seemed to summon up spirits. From the bells ringing in the small chapel he knew it was seven, the time at which the gate was locked. He suddenly remembered the time they had closed the cemetery with a visitor inside. It wasn't a story, it had happened to an acquaintance of his father.

Seized with horror, he fled the cemetery in the direction of the village. Upon reaching the corner of his street, he thought he made out a figure beneath the fading lamplight. Without hurrying, he continued on his way. The figure was a man waiting, leaning against the door of his house. Judging by his slightly stooped appearance, he seemed worn out, as though having waited for some time. Broyz realized it was Mister Roger.

"I came to ask a favour," said the Englishman.

"A favour?"

"Yes, I've been thinking it over. I'm prepared to pay a good sum of money."

Apparently, a famous architect in Lisbon was interested in Fernanda's bracelet, having received a description from the Englishman by post.

"I need you to inform the lady of my latest offer."

Broyz was astonished the Englishman was proposing to talk about the specific subject of that bracelet.

"Look, Mister Roger, just for today, I don't want to talk about that bracelet," he apologized, without giving any further explanation.

"I'm very sorry but the bracelet is the only way of settling the debt."

"What are you talking about?"

"About the debt your father incurred with me before his death," answered the art expert, showing some documents in which Broyz recognized the signature of his father at the bottom.

Broyz wanted to know why the Englishman had allowed two years to pass without reclaiming anything. The answer was immediate: it was the bracelet, not the money, that he really wanted.

"I'm very sorry," said Mister Roger for the second time. "You will speak to her, won't you?"

Broyz had no means to repay the debt. The Englishman only had to pressure him guilefully.

"Won't you?" he repeated, putting on his hat. He then rapped the knob of his cane twice in the palm of his left hand.

"Alright … I'll try and talk to her," Broyz said, "but I doubt she'll change her mind."

On Wednesday morning Broyz dressed in his finest clothes and headed for the castle. Each day of the previous week, he'd informed Fernanda that, come Wednesday, he would present her with a ring to make their engagement official. "If you accept the ring, Fernanda," Broyz told her, "it will mean that you accept to become my wife."

They both looked forward to the day with a sense of nervousness, but something had changed in Broyz following his visit to the cemetery. His love for the widow had not diminished, only now he judged it impossible that she would give herself to him in the same way as she had given herself to Antunes. "*The two of us for ever*," still echoed in his head. If Fernanda truly loved him, she ought to relinquish that bracelet, he concluded. In that way, he would resolve two problems at one stroke: the shadow of the deceased and the debt of his father.

Walking along the riverbank, the widow seemed anxious for Broyz to offer her the ring. However, after the shock of his visit to the cemetery, Broyz had decided to save himself the expenditure for the simple reason he didn't have any money to pay for it. The engagement day had arrived, yet it was a bracelet rather than a ring that preoccupied Broyz.

"There's something …" Broyz begun, clearing his throat. "There's something I must say to you."

The widow opened her eyes wide and Broyz started to talk, unable to control the flow of his words. First he said the wedding could not take place until she was parted from that bracelet. Next, he felt bound to admit to his trip to the tomb of the deceased, his only way of knowing about the twin bracelet. Finally, the conversation turned to the will, and the widow, red with rage, delivered an unexpected tirade in defence of Antunes Coelho: how dare Broyz reject the money earned by her late husband in such an irreproachable fashion; how could he be so insolent as to doubt the generosity of the dead man; how dare he ask her to get rid of that bracelet, the very same one that only a few months before he had found so "elegant". Even she did not understand how this dispute had evolved, but it was too late for apologies. And so Broyz snatched his hat from her grasp and departed in haste, leaving her halfway through a sentence.

Two months after that altercation, a servant knocked at Broyz's door. "I bring a letter from the senhora," he said. It dawned on Broyz that eight weeks had passed since he last saw Fernanda. He'd heard rumours she was ill, and others of a mysterious epidemic that made no distinction between rich and poor. He asked the servant if it was true the lady was bed-ridden. "I'm afraid it's true, senhor. What's more, she's so weak she no longer holds her pen and had to dictate the letter to a servant who knows how to write." Broyz unfolded the letter and read in silence by the flicker of candlelight. It demanded his urgent presence, but in such an amicable way that Broyz was led to believe, at that moment, that Fernanda had changed her mind and was finally ready for a fresh meeting.

They crossed the village in a carriage that bore the old family coat of arms emblazoned on its hood, the same arms that Broyz had admired in the cemetery. Galloping through barking dogs, they reached the castle gardens which, that summer, were flooded with a resplendent sea of wild yellow flowers, though a shade of greenish yellow that barely differed from the colour of the leaves and branches. Broyz grabbed a bunch. By the time he had entered the bedroom where the widow lay, and stood before that bed draped in linen, the flowers had already wilted. Perhaps it was the sense of luxury, or the fine scent of incense, or even some peculiar quality particular to those wild flowers, but the fact remained, the flowers were finished. They appeared like a discarded paper streamer and exuded an acrid smell that upset the widow, triggering a bout of sneezes. Seeing her nose wrinkle and her nostrils flair, Broyz ejected the dead bunch through the open window, picturing a heavy fall for those faded flowers.

As he was about to be seated on the widow's enormous bed, Broyz calculated how many people could fit on such a mattress. It was the biggest he'd ever seen in his life, despite his earlier years as a doctor's apprentice when he had come across hundreds, even thousands, of beds of all sizes, in which always lay some ailing person whose temperature he would check, or to whom he would give an injection, or examine their throat. However, this room in which he and Fernanda were meeting once more, inspired in him an exaggerated sense of respect, the sort awakened before a tomb. Had it not been for the widow lying between the sheets that sense of respect would not have been as great, since the aura of reverence resided not in the furniture, nor the carpets, nor the polished floorboards, but in her, Fernanda, in the way she looked at him eight weeks later to say, "I've thought it over, you treated me cruelly, but I don't care anymore," and he understood she was referring to the bracelet and his opinions about the deceased Antunes Coelho.

"I've thought it over, Broyz. You were a little harsh that other afternoon by the river, but I know it wasn't malice, but sincerity on your part, and because of that I ask you forgive me if I was quick tempered with you during our discussion."

Broyz said nothing.

"I've called you here to make a very important proposition: let's get married, Broyz. You've asked me more than once and now I accept, but our wedding will not be like any other. For it to happen, you must listen with the utmost attention."

Broyz said nothing.

"You are very aware I don't love you, Broyz. But I realize I'm caught in a trap and I want to escape it."

Broyz said that he, for his part, did love her.

"What I suggest, Broyz, is that if you do love me, then marry me, live for a time in this house, cover up appearances, ignore the gossips, but after a while go away and don't come back. I offer you one third of the castle's possessions. It's not what's stipulated in the will, but it's still more than you could amass in seven lifetimes."

Broyz said nothing, stunned by the proposal.

"Only by marrying someone like you can I ensure that my former husband's fortune will not end up in the hands of some shameless person."

Broyz told her she could be sure of many more things.

"Another thing, Broyz, after a while you'll leave, having taken your share of the money."

Broyz said he would accept only on one condition:

"You must remove your bracelet and hand it to me. On our wedding day, I'll bring you a shining gold ring."

"That's your condition?" she asked, suppressing her laughter.

Broyz replied in all seriousness that it was.

There was a brief silence which, to Broyz, lasted an eternity, before being broken when Fernanda said:

"Okay, Broyz. Here, it's yours."

The church bells chimed three when Mister Roger knocked at Broyz's door with the knob of his cane. Both blows resonated in almost perfect unison.

"Well done. I already know you've obtained it," said the

Englishman, who was wearing a heavy suit, too thick and bulky for the climate.

For some days Vila Natal had been overwhelmed by such heat that the daily life of the villagers had changed: many took long siestas after midday; others worked at night, beneath the pale light of the stars. Only a few could stand the heat, and Broyz was surprised that Mister Roger was one of them, bearing in mind his advanced years.

"You're mistaken," Broyz corrected. "It wasn't for you I obtained the bracelet."

" Not for me … then you've forgotten the debt."

"The debt! Of course … Let's settle up right away," responded Broyz, holding forth a wad of banknotes that Mister Roger looked at in bewilderment. "Take this money, please. Count it."

"It's not necessary and well you know it. What's more, I'm ready to cancel your debt if you just tell me where to find the bracelet and how you obtained this money."

"Are you serious?"

Consumed by curiosity, Mister Roger took the documents bearing Ricardo Broyz's signature and slowly began to rip them apart, holding one end of each page firmly with one hand and tearing with the other.

And so Broyz told him that two days before, early in the morning, he'd called on a pawnshop in Coimbra. The money-lender had accepted the bracelet as a guarantee, handing him in exchange just enough money to pay off the debt and buy the ring.

"Fernanda mustn't find out about this," Broyz warned. The Englishman made a gesture to indicate he could be counted on.

Once married to the widow, Broyz continued, he would return to Coimbra and recover the bracelet, paying the money-lender with some other object he would manage to sneak from the castle, the absence of which would, by contrast, pass unnoticed.

"Bravo … very clever," said the Englishman.

"Don't exaggerate. Now tell me how you knew I had the bracelet."

"That's easily explained, my dear Broyz. On the same day you travelled to Coimbra, I plucked up the courage to return to the castle with a new offer. To my surprise, your wife-to-be listened with great interest. Go and see Broyz, she said, and pay him the price we've agreed for the bracelet."

Broyz looked at the Englishman in utter disbelief.

"Do you expect me …"

"You don't believe me?" protested Mister Roger. "She received me in her bed because she was ill. She dictated this card to a servant named Fabio, and signed at the bottom. Isn't this her signature?"

Broyz had to admit that it was. He then read quietly, to himself: "*In order to prove to you, Broyz, that I wish to seal our pact, that the bracelet no longer retains any significance, I've agreed this very day to sell it to Mister Roger, a man in whom I have complete trust and who is an old friend of your father. I ask you to hand over the bracelet in return for …*"

"Now do you believe me?" boasted the Englishman.

The new offer was six times greater than the sum paid by the moneylender in Coimbra. The widow suggested Broyz share the dividends equally, even though the bracelet was not part of the inheritance.

"Dear Broyz," said Mister Roger, "I await your next journey to Coimbra. If you retrieve the bracelet, you know where to find me. The offer still stands."

CHAPTER THREE

F RIAR EMILIO was the superior at the monastery in Caminhos.
He was a small man, almost without shoulders, stooped
beneath his worn soutane, and with a shrill voice that everyone
described as being like a bird's cry. In spite of this seeming
weakness, he was a hardened character and had resolved to
install electricity in the monastery against the wishes of some
parishioners and many priests from neighbouring parishes.
"A light that's effective but austere," were the instructions Luís
Agua had received from Friar Emilio. Together they evaluated
the plans and settled on a period of two to four months for the
completion of the work.

Agua imagined his arrival in Caminhos would be something
of an event, not only because of the novelty of electricity, but
also because the cloister where the friars lived would not have
been likely to provide them with many opportunities to talk
with strangers. Nevertheless, to his surprise, the friars knew
everything about the neighbouring villages and were up to date
with news about the recent auction at the castle. They even
knew Senhora Fernanda from the days when she and Antunes
Coelho were benefactors of the monastery.

It was during those days spent in Caminhos that Agua learnt
of the plague spreading through the poorest villages in the
central region of the country. "The danger's greater than the
authorities in Coimbra would lead us to believe," Friar Emilio
confessed one evening. Agua couldn't contain his amazement.
What did these friars who lived on the fringes of society know
about life outside their walls? "Come, follow me," said the friar
when they had finished their evening meal, and he led Agua
through a labyrinth of descending passages that terminated at
a battered wooden door.

"We cannot enter, it's dangerous," said Friar Emilio, "but
listen carefully, do you hear the groans?" It was true. From the
other side came the sound of wailing which seemed to seep
through the crack in the door. "There are eighty-five. Last month

there were fifty, but more arrive all the time. Of course, their families are afraid of being infected, and the doctors don't know what to prescribe. It's an unknown and exotic disease. Shall we go back?"

Luís Agua did not have a good night. Every half hour he awoke convinced he heard in his room a sinister litany rising from beneath his bed. To compound matters, the oppressive heat prevented him from further sleep. Next day he asked Friar Emilio for more details about the disease. How was it contracted? The friar didn't know, although he had heard a doctor say the livestock was infected and the milk from the cows dangerous unless boiled before drinking. How many other villages in the central region risked infection? The friar was unable to answer. The conversation turned to Vila Natal and Agua wondered if the disease could spread that far. Friar Emilio offered a sardonic smile. "Vila Natal?" he mused. "Oh, it would be justice itself if the pestilence had the gift of modifying Friar Teresino's outdated ideas … but, goodness, forgive me Lord for being so spiteful towards one of your fellow servants."

After Caminhos, Agua did not return to Coimbra directly, but stopped off in Leiria, and then Batalha, towns where electrical works were in progress. Once back in Coimbra, he began to prepare for his move to Vila Natal. He advised the owner of the boarding-house that he wouldn't be renewing his contract at the end of the month, drew up a report with all the latest news for the central office of Douglas & Banks in Lisbon, and went out for a last walk in Coimbra to bid farewell to a few cafés and corners of the town that he would surely miss once settled in Vila Natal.

"The only thing I'll miss in this city are it's cafés and nightlife," he thought, just as a young man, who looked like a down-and-out, intercepted his path and stuffed some leaflets into his hand. Agua continued walking and stopped at a bar to drink a glass of wine. Only as he left the bar, at the foot of the Almedina arch, did he glance at the leaflets. His eyes widened as he read its title: *The Encyclopaedia of Bottoms* by Dr Broyz, second edition.

"Stop," he said to a lad who was ambling past. "Tell me, is this well known?"

"*The Encyclopaedia*," laughed the boy, revealing a set of discoloured and chipped teeth. "Yes, it's very popular at the University. The first edition, two weeks ago, was a hit with the students. Somebody's distributing a second edition round the city, but the rector has promised to punish the miscreant."

"*This is, dear reader, a complete catalogue of bottoms written by an expert in injections who has had more sightings of that region of the human anatomy than a public latrine,*" read Agua. There then followed something like a classification of bottoms, written in the customary satirical style appropriate to students, though with a poetic touch that Agua noticed was very much in keeping with the grandiloquent manifestos being recited in the big cities at that period. The catalogue listed:

. . . firm and round ones that recall oranges
firm ones that broaden out to recall pears
ones that broaden upwards to recall guitars
flabby ones
gelatinous ones
ones firm around the hip, softening at the thigh
ones pitted like craters
athletic ones, always taut and ready to run
ones with a big spot that invite an injection right there
ones that tremble at the impending injection
ones that contract at the impending injection
small and snub ones
ones sunken into the flesh, like a desert island
ones for kissing
ones for biting
ones for licking
ones for caressing
ones for slapping
ones for fondling
ones for kicking
ones for whipping
immaculate ones

bruised ones
scratched ones
ticklish ones
insensitive ones
speckled ones
twisting ones
throbbing ones
cold ones
frozen ones, always
hot blushing ones
creamy ones
fatty ones
shiny like wax ones
plump ones
slippery ones
clumsy ones
funny ones
common ones
exotic ones
opulent ones
diminutive ones
touchable ones
arthritic ones
spongy ones
coarse ones
velvety ones
ones soft to the touch that recall peaches
ones with hair so fair it's not seen
ones with dark hair that clouds its charm
ones with hair at the base, akin to a beard
ones with hair around the anus
ones with a big anus the size of an eye
ones with an anus shut tight
ones with folds, like a double chin
ones with fan folds
ones with smooth folds
wounded ones

vigorous ones
asymmetrical ones with one cheek bigger
asymmetrical ones with one cheek sagging
ones that end in a point, like an elbow
ones with small spots
ones with boils
ones with scars
ones with freckles
square ones
white ones
pink ones, like a baby's
yellowish ones
greyish ones
sun-roasted ones
pale ones
ruddy ones that recall apples
ones of an unpredictable shape
elevated ones
fallen ones
curled ones
enormous ones
uncontainable ones
robust ones
delicate ones
ones with burn marks
ones with itches
ones with rashes
ones that appear to have burst from their underwear
ones that appear to have collapsed from their underwear
ones striated with veins like rivers on maps
smelly ones
repugnant ones
dirty ones . . .

"Broyz? Was it possible?" thought Agua. Something told him the Broyz he'd met at the auction was incapable of writing something like that.

Servants at the foot of the bed. The registrar. Dogs barking in the park. The marriage between Broyz and Fernanda was no more than a brief formality with few witnesses. She hadn't enough strength to rise from her bed, even though she promised Broyz and those who wished to listen that come the wedding she would be in good health.

When the registrar finished the customary proceedings, a strange sound flew through the bedroom and the servants rushed to the window. An aeroplane was preparing to land in the castle grounds.

The servants escorted Broyz as he raced towards the park, where a man dressed in turquoise overalls awaited them. His hands were crossed across his stomach as he peered skywards, as if unable to believe he'd just come from there.

"Who else came with you in the aeroplane?" asked Broyz, coming to a halt.

The aviator, until then holding a pose with his fingers linked, reacted by staring intently at Broyz.

"Who else came?" he repeated. "All of us!" And he gestured wildly towards the empty park behind him.

Broyz was slow to pick up the joke, until the aviator spat on the lawn and chuckled disagreeably.

"My aeroplane is a one-seater and I've come alone. Allow me to introduce myself. I'm Captain Alfredo Acevedo. I hope I'm not late for the wedding … the journey was a little …"

Acevedo broke off abruptly. He'd just noticed the suit Broyz wore and thus deduced he was talking to the future husband.

"You are … you must be …" Acevedo wavered, and from his overalls he plucked a crumpled piece of paper. He spread it on the palm of his left hand.

"You are Senhor Broyz," he said, spelling out the name as though pronouncing it for the first time, as perhaps he was.

At this juncture in the conversation the servants weren't crowded around the plane as Broyz would have imagined. The captain had landed at the castle on previous occasions, he surmised, hence their familiarity with the machine.

"Is it yours?"

"Of course it's mine. I used all my savings buying it. Take a look if you wish. Come closer. Touch it. It's a Blériot, made in France. Soon, you know, carts will be a thing of the past and there'll be only automobiles and aeroplanes on this planet. And so I said to myself, why wait for that day to arrive? Why not anticipate progress? I'm not young like you … I mean, you'll be able to fly when you're my age, but I can't wait that long."

"I presume you bought it over there, in France."

"You're quite right. I brought it from Paris, landing every now and then to refuel. Would you like to fly with me?"

"I don't understand, captain. You just said there was only space for one person."

"I said there's only one seat, that's not the same thing. If you want to fly, we could arrange ourselves. You'd have to sit at my knees. Don't laugh … you wouldn't be the first that …"

"I beg your pardon, but how did you know about our wedding? Are you a friend or relation of Fernanda?"

"I'm like one of the family. Antunes Coelho and I were inseparable … what you might call childhood brothers. Ah, what times we had! I'm not a young man anymore, you know, although I've managed to keep myself in good shape."

Broyz nodded.

"Ah, don't imagine that just because I was a friend of the deceased, this wedding doesn't give me pleasure. On the contrary, quite the opposite. I'm no longer a young lad, but I understand these traditions of remarrying. A woman needs a man to love her. I congratulate you, senhor …" and again the future husband's name slipped his memory.

"Broyz," said Broyz.

"Yes, senhor, I congratulate you. And now, with your permission," said Acevedo, bowing, "I shall go and greet Senhora Fernanda. She had the kindness to invite me."

After instructing the servants to accompany the captain to the bedroom, Broyz approached the aeroplane, filled with curiosity. He was inspecting it when a deep voice startled him from behind.

"Has the registrar finished?"

It was Friar Teresino, who was waiting impatiently for his moment to unite Broyz and Fernanda before God.

"He's finished, Father. Come with me," said Broyz, who wished to continue with the ceremony. However, the widow and the aviator were talking in the bedroom, behind closed doors, and had given strict instructions that nobody should disturb them.

When their confinement stretched to half an hour, Broyz became impatient. What were they talking about? And why were they doing so in secret, without him? Eventually, the door opened and the friar was able to give his benediction to the newly-weds. Fernanda immediately claimed a headache and demanded everyone leave her bedroom, everyone except for her new spouse.

The captain bade farewell to Broyz and Fernanda, then to the servants, giving each in turn a firm handshake, as though he was heading into battle. After taking off, he steered the aeroplane in the direction of the river; then turned and started making circles. Finally, he traced a figure of eight and turned back again towards the castle. Perhaps he had forgotten something.

"Look," a servant shouted, pointing above a tree.

The little plane was expelling a thick white cloud and seemed to be writing in the sky.

"Is it a *D*?"

"It's an *O*."

The smoke rapidly dispersed, leaving the servants in disagreement over what letters the captain trailed.

As the aeroplane drew away, going full throttle, so the engine noise faded and an imposing silence fell once more on the castle.

Acevedo disappeared amid the scattered clouds, and the married couple hid away in the bedroom, the key turned in the lock. They remained there for three days, during which time they sought food twice only. Meanwhile, the servants slaved away, transforming the rest of the house as agreed with their masters: they waxed the floors, painted the walls with fresh colours, refurbished the furniture, reorganized the paintings, made cushions, embroidered tablecloths and polished cutlery.

Broyz emerged three days later, somewhat unshaven, to discover an unrecognizable landscape cast before his eyes. He and
the widow were both extremely satisfied with the work of the
servants, though Broyz didn't recall giving instructions for a
large portrait of Antunes Coelho to be hung in the entrance
hall. A little disconcerted, he voiced a mild protest. The servants replied the painting had always been there, since well
before he arrived. "Have I passed before this portrait without
noticing it? That's impossible," Broyz reflected as he crossed
the drawing room and stood on tiptoes to touch the painting.
He ran his index along the bushy moustache, the forehead
etched with a single furrow running deep between the brows to
bury itself at the point where the large nose began. He traced
the jaw and the hint of a double chin. The corpulence of
Antunes amazed him. He had the girth of a wearied man, not
a healthy person overfed at the most magnificent banquets.
The decanter, clock, goblets, various books, snuffbox, pipes, an
old gun and two small porcelain vases, all objects appreciated
by the deceased during his lifetime, were arranged on a low
table. If a few days earlier they had seemed lifeless, now they
shone anew beneath the portrait, displayed as an offering to
their old master.

A month after the wedding, the widow asked Broyz if Mister
Roger had paid him the agreed price for the bracelet.
Surprised by the question, Broyz didn't know how to reply, and
a look of panic flashed across his face. "We're in the process of
concluding the deal …" he started to say, searching for words.
Suddenly the excuse occurred to him. He was still holding the
bracelet because he wanted to obtain an even higher price
from the Englishman. "That's better," Fernanda uttered. "You
can't imagine how relieved I am to hear that." It transpired the
widow regretted fixing a price for the bracelet, for now she was
married, she had free access to the inheritance and had no
need for money. And, in any case, she had too many senti-
mental ties linking her to the bracelet.

For several days they spoke no further about the matter. The widow believed Broyz's story and didn't seek to reclaim the jewel. Yet Broyz could not fully trust the moneylender who had sworn to keep hold of the bracelet. Thus, a short while later, he informed Fernanda of his intent to leave for Coimbra in search of a specialist doctor for her illness. The rector of the University would know whom to recommend. As the only other doctor in the whole of Vila Natal was Dr Gonçalves, an old man already retired because of his trembling hands, Broyz's pretext for travel was both valid and ingenious.

It mustn't be concluded that by undertaking this escapade Broyz was reconsidering his interest in medicine. No, that was a finished matter. His father had forced him to study that branch of science and he'd responded by obtaining outstanding qualifications. But his father's death had drawn an end to the whole farce. Medicine was not his true vocation, so much so that the diploma obtained at the end still remained uncollected at the University and meant little to him.

On the journey to Coimbra, he determined he would make no reference to the diploma during his meeting at the University. He would not reclaim it, not unless the rector mentioned it.

He dedicated his first day to the retrieval of the bracelet, giving the moneylender a cameo brooch and a small dagger with a silver hilt by way of recompense. On the second day, relieved at having already recuperated the jewel, he made his way through the bustling corridors of the University in search of the dark and silent library. He received a strange thrill returning there after such a long time.

He spent the whole afternoon buried in books, the same ones he had memorized for his exams. An appointment with the rector, Dom Enrique Jardim de Vilhena, was arranged for the end of the day. In the meantime, he had ample time in which to check those works, in search of a similar case to the one that had laid Fernanda low. If only he could leave Coimbra with a diagnosis … (There were only torturous seats without backs in the library, but he wasn't about to abandon his mission for that reason.) He finished pouring over the books. Out of four possible diseases, he noted one, cholera. The other three options were scarcely more delightful.

His eyes scanned the old pages of the *Vindicae Medicinae et Medicorum* and Thomas Brooks' *Heavenly Cordiel*, in which was the recommendation to burn cedar wood rather than coal in order to purify the air where the disease could be lying dormant. "*Other ancient remedies can also be tried*," he continued reading, "*such as washing the head with vinegar, or placing a clove of garlic in the mouth, or applying coarse vinegar to the marks on the skin.*"

Cholera! Cholera! The name of the disease resounded in his head. He tried to calm himself and left the library, headed for the courtyard fountain situated between the classrooms. How was it possible the widow could have contracted cholera? Could it be a consequence of blood transfusions in the past recommended by Dr Gonçalves?

The rector received him after a short wait. He had aged considerably. Where before he had fat rosy cheeks, he now displayed maroon-coloured cheekbones. He was scarcely recognizable. And to make matters worse, he coughed incessantly. The secretary had warned Broyz, while he waited, not to smoke during the interview. For his own sake, Broyz decided to keep silent during the coughing fits. He sensed the rector heard nothing, the noise of his cough being so loud it drowned the words of others. Even so, Broyz managed to say he'd come because he urgently needed a doctor for his wife.

"It's just as well you've come," said the rector, reaching for a copy of *The Encyclopaedia of Bottoms*, the existence of which Broyz was, of course, ignorant.

Scarcely had Broyz read a few lines than he began to pale. "Who's the author of this rubbish? Who has the effrontery to use my name, to make ridicule of it in such a way?" he asked, feeling a mixture of impotence and indignation.

"Calm down, my dear Broyz. I know all too well you didn't write this barbarity. You wouldn't be so foolish as to attach your own name," said Jardim, with difficulty, between bouts of coughing.

With regards to Senhora Antunes Coelho's illness, he asked

Broyz to describe the symptoms. Broyz had just begun to list a few when a worried expression drew across the rector's face.

"African fever …" he spluttered from behind his desk, then coughed.

Broyz had never heard talk of African fever because it was a secret subject only debated within the scientific circles of Coimbra and Lisbon.

In 1888, Portugal had witnessed the confirmation of her colonial sovereignty in African territories, such as Angola and Mozambique. Since then, many ships had set sail from the port of Lisbon heading for the colonies, returning to Lisbon and then back to the colonies, taking out adventurers, bringing back Zulu slaves as well as Egyptian, Dutch or Indian emigrants who had tried their luck in the colonies and were coming back to Portugal, a few of them rich, but most poor. All this traffic from the Subtropics to the Old Continent had placed the Portuguese in contact with a world of mystery and savagery.

The rector explained, between coughing fits, that African fever was another consequence of the many voyages, especially in recent history, after the end of the Great War, when many colonials had chosen to return to Europe. On the homeward bound journeys, in ships crammed full, veritable floating cities without hygiene, they had contracted all manner of infections. According to Jardim, when the government learnt that lack of maritime health was responsible for transporting epidemics from Africa, it tried to prevent those ships disembarking in Lisbon. Obligatory quarantine was decreed. As soon as ships docked, maritime police and medical experts in exotic diseases subjected travellers as well as crew members to inspection. Those suspected of being contagious were forced to remain on board. A yellow or red flag was hoisted, according to the seriousness of the outbreak, quarantine regularly exceeding two months.

Despite these precautions, said Jardim, African fever was decimating Portugal. In Lisbon some cases had been controlled in time, but the greatest danger of infection was in rural parts, among the malnourished peasants as well as the landowners.

When the rector finished his explanation, Broyz was left at a loss for words. Fernanda had African fever? It seemed absurd, but he listened in silence as the rector continued:

"I know a young doctor, a specialist in African fever." Cough. "He often passes through the region." Cough. "I'll ask him to call at the castle."

For reasons that can only be explained as chance, at the same time as Broyz travelled from Vila Natal to Coimbra, along the same road, but venturing in the opposite direction, another carriage was transporting Luís Agua from Coimbra to the village. It goes without saying both travellers crossed paths without realizing, and it would be highly likely that, at the very moment of crossing, both Agua and Broyz were fast asleep.

In order to leave his boarding-house in Coimbra, Agua decided to lie to his supervisors in Lisbon, writing to inform them that, in the village called Vila Natal ("*the very one you believed to be non-existent*"), they required his services to pave the way for the imminent inauguration, of a commercial street, a short Avenue of Light that would enhance the village's tourist appeal and allow the wine growers to organize a festival during the grape harvest, at which they could sell their best produce.

Pure make-believe on Agua's part, this Avenue of Light was no more than one of the many projects he wanted to propose to Mister Roger and the influential men of the village as soon as he was settled. However, before instigating any proposals, he had to bide his time, for the completion of his move would inevitably take a while. Apart from the luggage he brought with him, Agua had parcelled and freighted three trunks whose arrival had been delayed: the largest contained the rest of his personal belongings; the two smaller ones, looking almost identical, contained work tools in one and miniature ships that he bottled as a hobby in the other. He waited impatiently for the arrival of this luggage, agreed for that week with a travel firm in Coimbra.

The first initiative he took, having arrived at his new village, was to visit Friar Teresino and offer to install electricity for the parish church. He had learnt this strategy from the company and applied it in every village in which his initial demonstration hadn't had the desired effects. It was generally the case that once the wealthy men of the village had seen the church illuminated, they would decide to engage his services. But even if Agua usually illuminated the church as a present after having exhausted other less expensive promotional resources available to him, in this case, as he was eager to settle in Vila Natal, he dispensed with the recommendations and proposed the benefits of electric light to the friar in exchange for his help in convincing the villagers of the usefulness of an electric installation.

The priest, who spoke in private the same way as during his sermons, replied that that whole invention was not really to his liking.

"Light, my son, comes from God … and if God wanted there to be only the light of day, it's because he reserved night for rest and prayer. Are you suggesting my parishioners approve … or, worse still, succumb to an invention of the devil?"

Agua could not convince the friar to modify his beliefs, which he considered outdated. But that wasn't the end of the matter. The friar began to reproach him for seeking collaboration ("it's not good Christian behaviour to make a gift to the Church with conditions attached"), just at the very moment an altar-boy burst into the room to announce that Fabio, the butler from Antunes Coelho's castle, requested to see him on Senhora Fernanda's behalf.

"Of course, of course … let him in right away," the friar urged, forgetting Agua's presence.

"Father," said the servant, entering. "The senhora is very ill and mumbles your name. I fear she's in need of extreme unction."

"Good Lord! I'm coming at once."

"Thank you, Father. I've brought a carriage to take you."

Without saying goodbye, the friar left the church almost running. Agua followed him into the street, hoisted his case onto his shoulder and headed off towards Mister Roger's house. He walked fifty or a hundred metres and stopped, exhausted. Then he started again. After a little while he discovered the Englishman's house was not where he vaguely remembered it to be. In fact, the houses in the village were so alike it became almost impossible to distinguish one from another.

That detour only served to demoralize him. He came across so many tumbledown houses, all alike, that he began to suspect he would never find a house in the village for himself that was comfortable and in good condition. Besides Mister Roger's house, barely three or four others stood out in the overall landscape. He decided to knock from door to door at the elegant houses until he found the Englishman. In Vila Natal, however, it was customary to treat all strangers with mistrust. "Mister Roger? No, he's in the other street," a servant informed him. "Mister Roger? No, he doesn't live here," a maidservant said, and she deliberately pointed him towards a house that was not the Englishman's, but the notary's. "Mister Roger? No senhor," said the notary himself. Noticing Agua was staggering beneath the weight of his case, he invited him in and introduced him to his nephew and secretary.

"I think I can guess who you are," said the notary's nephew before Agua had had an opportunity to introduce himself. "I don't remember your name, but I know what you do … Mister Roger comes here talking about the arrival of electricity and the young man who carries a small lighting factory on his shoulder."

"Good … but, in truth, it's not really a factory," Agua explained, and both turned to smile at the notary.

CHAPTER FOUR

"Is she still ill?" Friar Teresino asked the chamber-maid who accompanied him upstairs to the bedroom.

"She's so pale, she's unrecognizable. Just before the wedding, she seemed to have recovered, but now she spends the afternoons crying when she's not sleeping for long periods."

They continued in silence. Fabio escorted them, a few steps ahead, pretending not to be listening to the conversation. On arrival, another chamber-maid jumped forward.

"Thank heavens!" she exclaimed. "Come in, Father. This way. We were beginning to think you weren't coming."

Fernanda was asleep, upright and leaning back on a large pillow. The sound of her breathing echoed as though from afar. Friar Teresino signed the air with a blessing and asked all present, including Fabio, to leave the room.

The widow awoke with a start when the priest took hold of her hand.

"Father! Forgive me for calling you, but I haven't the strength to attend church."

Her kind and somewhat haughty voice was now so faint that Friar Teresino had to sit close on the bed and bend his shaven head towards her.

The widow, filled with remorse for having married Broyz, wanted to make a confession. Something said her hours were numbered. She had agreed to the wedding to gain access to her husband's fortune. Though now she felt the presence of death, and saw her fortune winding up in Broyz's hands, she wished she'd never given him her bracelet or ever allowed him into the castle.

"Understand me, Father," she murmured.

The friar presented a host, which she kept on her tongue for a few seconds.

"*Corpus Domini nostri … In vitam aeternam …*" recited Father Teresino, a trace of pride adding conviction to his words.

"Thank you," said Fernanda.

He kissed her forehead before withdrawing. The widow fell back to sleep, this time with a serene smile. When she awoke, she gathered together her servants and maids at the foot of her bed and informed them that Senhor Broyz's belongings should be removed from her bedroom.

The servants were secretly delighted for, since the wedding, their freedom was being curtailed. Until Broyz's arrival, they had dedicated themselves to sowing and harvesting the lands around the park, as agreed with Fernanda following Antunes' death.

"My husband has passed away. In order to ration the small sum of money that still belongs to me, I'm going to part with you all, except for a butler and a cook," the newly-widowed woman had informed them in 1911. And so, the servants, as always lead by Fabio, made a bold counter-proposal: "We shall stay here, tilling the lands, milking the cows and goats. You'll have food thanks to our farming, and we, in turn, will receive lodgings and a share of the harvest." And thus, in such manner, Fernanda had contrived to retain an entourage of servants and maids, far too many even for a wealthy nobleman.

Now with the powers he gained following the wedding, Broyz was trying to modify the agreement, as the servants were only too well aware.

"Fernanda, dearest," he said, voicing his opinion. "The lands are now legally ours. We should pay the servants for their work and optimize the profits."

But the widow preferred to leave things as they were, partly out of gratitude to her faithful servants, and partly not to give in to Broyz, from whom she awaited nothing more than a prompt departure.

And so, upon his return from Coimbra, and after returning the bracelet to the widow, Broyz discovered his belongings had been transferred to a room at the top of the battlement tower. He tried to protest, but Fernanda reminded him of their marriage pact and argued further that she needed rest.

"You can use the room in the tower, Broyz. You can wear my husband's clothes. However, let me remind you that in a couple of weeks you must go. That's what we agreed."

Broyz couldn't believe his ears. She had said "my husband," referring to the late Antunes. She had ignored him. All she expected was that he should leave with his share of the fortune.

"I'm sorry," he replied, "but I will not leave until I see you restored to health."

And so, he did as he said. When the doctor promised by Jardim de Vilhena didn't arrive, Broyz felt obliged to stay at the widow's bedside. He kept vigil for entire afternoons, applying wet flannels to her fevered brow, never worrying that when she opened her eyes she would reiterate: "Leave, Broyz, you mustn't stay here."

Fernanda's litany comprised: *you must go—leave me alone—leave by night if you don't want to be seen—remember the agreement—don't stay by my side—I don't want to see you here tomorrow.*

Broyz's response litany comprised: *how are you feeling—I can't leave you in this state—you must rest—I'll go later, I'm in no hurry—I'll uphold the agreement but your health comes first—I love you—I'll go next week—don't be upset, sleep.*

Nothing could alter Broyz's determination, not even the servants who passed right in front of his eyes, ignoring him, turning deaf ears to his orders, bringing meals and teas for the senhora and nothing for him. No matter how distant his room in the tower may have been, there was no reason for him to be abandoned in such a manner.

Certainly, Broyz gave them no orders. There was a sense of fear in his attitude towards them. Another man might have imposed himself by raising his voice, but he wasn't predisposed to that sort of behaviour. On the contrary, it cost him dear to fetch his food when the servants pretended to forget him.

Likewise with his clothes. As time passed, against his wishes, he had to resort to entering the wardrobe of the late Antunes Coelho. None of the servants washed the shirts, socks or trousers left by Broyz in the wicker basket, where the senhora's dirty bed linen was discarded. Every morning when he raised its lid, he discovered his clothes had disappeared, but he dared not ask for them back.

"Well, here I am in a suit belonging to Antunes Coelho. For

a moment, I don't feel worthy of wearing it, and so it's hardly a surprise my body feels so insignificant when this jacket seems so baggy. Perhaps, if I told the servants whom the suit belonged to, they would show a modicum of respect," reflected Broyz, as he wandered wearily around the castle. He was half-empty, without consistency in his ill-fitting attire. This state of insubstantiality, however, had more to do with the result of his hunger.

There had been so many maids and servants he'd never managed to remember all their names and often discovered a new face. So, on the night he met Alma, he'd gone down to the kitchens earlier than usual because his hunger was unbearable. "I'm tired, but I suspect I won't sleep tonight until I've satisfied my appetite. Perhaps, I should do all the things that usually make me tired: shave, polish my shoes … no, today I won't have the necessary patience for those rituals," he thought, as a gleam from a lamp caught him by surprise. In the kitchen, a maid, who had just finished washing the plates and cutlery, was cleaning the fat from the pans.

"Excellent work," he complimented without expecting a response, accustomed to being ignored by everyone.

The young girl raised her face and gathered two locks of black hair falling over her eyes, turning them behind her ears.

"Would senhor like some old cloth?" she asked, smiling openly.

Broyz blushed. Perhaps the maid was making fun of him, seeing him in the deceased's clothes? Nothing was further from her mind: the girl was offering him a stew known as old cloth, made of tomatoes and left-over meat.

Broyz drew nearer, lured by the smell rising from the pot. Alma lit the fire to heat the old cloth; it made Broyz's mouth water.

"*A pot cooked in haste, looses its taste,*" recited the girl, in Spanish.

The stew would take a while before it was hot enough. It wasn't easy for Broyz to suppress his hunger.

"Listen, I'll serve your plate as soon as it's ready," said Alma, "but you mustn't stay here. It'd be better if I brought a helping to your room."

As a result of that meeting, not a lunch or dinner passed when Alma didn't slip him some food or cigarettes, always behind the backs of the other servants. Nobody knew she had broken the boycott.

The doctor sent by Jardim de Vilhena was called Xavier Alves. He appeared extremely competent. Nevertheless, despite his efforts, the widow's condition deteriorated. Confined to her bed, at times her skin turned completely blue as she crumpled on the verge of asphyxiation.

Broyz no longer knew where to turn. He considered going to the village to see Dr Gonzales, but then he remembered that on his last visit to the castle Friar Teresino had informed the widow of the old doctor's death. "I must stay calm and trust Alves," he told himself resolutely. "It's not fair to be jealous of another doctor when it concerns Fernanda's health."

Shut away in the battlement tower, Broyz found few opportunities to speak with Alves. One favourable occasion appeared as the doctor crossed the park, heading for his carriage to return to Vila Natal.

"One moment, Doctor," he shouted. Alves slowed.

Walking side by side, Broyz sought to confirm his suspicions concerning his wife's illness, though when the doctor heard him suggest an African fever, he gestured him to lower his voice.

"Yes, it's possible," he said, almost in a whisper, "but this disease mustn't be mentioned for the time being."

Very early the following day, Broyz awoke startled by a noise he imagined to be the pendulum clock, but which was in fact Fabio's footsteps as he impudently climbed the spiral staircase.

Broyz was lying on his back, covered from the waist down by a thin blanket, when Fabio pushed the door open with the toe of his shoe and walked across to the window. After drawing back the heavy curtain, he threw open the window, filling the room with bright light.

"Get out! Let me sleep!" Broyz ordered, shielding his eyes,

not from Fabio's intimidating gaze, but from the first rays of sunlight blinding him.

"The senhora sends me to ask if you're leaving today. If you wish to do so, there's a carriage at your disposal. Are you leaving, senhor?"

Broyz replied he was not. Fabio scratched his head, raised his eyebrows with disdain and thrice repeated the question "Are you leaving, senhor?" to which Broyz responded each time with the negative. Then, before withdrawing, he solemnly announced:

"Senhor Broyz, the senhora also instructs me to inform you that on Dr Alves's orders, nobody can enter her bedroom, not even you."

Evidently, Fabio was more than just a servant, perhaps even the widow's personal butler. He wore the same clothes as the others, the same old uniform, slightly worn, but nevertheless impeccable: gray trousers, black shoes, white shirt and an olive-green jacket. He had never revealed anything that might differentiate him from the other servants, but Broyz presumed Fernanda gave him preferential treatment. From that day, Fabio's early morning took on a regular pattern. He would always pose the same question and then listen to Broyz respond that he would not abandon the castle until the widow was restored to health. He would then take a step forward, a movement so precise as to suggest he rehearsed it at night, and impart fresh orders from the senhora: Broyz not only had to keep away from her bedroom, but also from the adjacent corridor; Broyz must not visit the bedrooms of the servants and maids; Broyz had no rights to demand food in the kitchen; Broyz was forbidden entrance to the small room behind the main hall, where a chamber-maid was certain she had seen him prowling.

"Me, prowling around a room on the ground floor? What are you talking about, Fabio?"

"You know very well what I'm talking about, senhor. I'm referring to the room which Senhor Antunes called the study. Since his death, it has remained in darkness, locked. No-one has set foot in it. You must not infringe on this practice."

It wasn't true. He had never paid particular attention to that room. But, as happens in these situations, the very act of prevention exercised a magnetism, and for one week, day and night, Broyz kept a close watch over every movement around the study until he began to suspect that Antunes Coelho was in reality alive, shut away in that room. His suspicions were based on the fact that, once or twice a day, a servant who had a key used to enter and leave with what appeared to be a plate of food. It was a very quick manoeuvre, and the servant took care to always visit the room at different hours of the day, as though making it seem haphazard.

Broyz didn't understand what was happening. Supposing Antunes had sought a new head of family to take care of finances and enable him to enjoy a retreat, hidden away in the confines of his study? Was it possible Fernanda would consent to something like that? Or perhaps she considered him dead and was unaware of all that occurred in the room?

Broyz soon found an explanation for the servant's routine and had to laugh at his vivid imagination: surviving in the study, old and unwell, was the cat that had belonged to Antunes. A servant named Hélio was feeding it, taking care it didn't escape into the park where the dogs would finish it off. The widow had invented the prohibitions of the study and the servants' rooms to enclose Broyz in the tower, to see if she could provoke his disgust in this way and hasten his departure. And while Broyz counted the interminable hours in his isolated tower, and while he tried to rest in his room with its tiny window which overlooked a corner of the garden where snarling dogs gathered at night preventing sleep, the servants and maids gathered together around the long table in the smoky kitchen and dedicated their time to two activities: chewing and conspiring. Reason revealed that after so much chewing they would begin to conspire, and because they conspired so much they never stopped chewing, thus transforming the chewing of tasty morsels into chewing against Broyz, and into chewing over their uncertainty with regard to the senhora, and into chewing over an elaborate plan to engulf that man who pretended to be their master, and even though he lacked an authoritative voice the servants maintained that that grasping man, that meddling man, that man … that man … and so the accusations lurched onwards around that wooden table.

Broyz seemed like the helpless guest taken in one stormy day, but he was the new master of the place. He seemed like the hideous relative locked away secretly in an attic, but he had married a woman now instructing him to leave, sending down her messages through Fabio.

"The senhora has estimated how much corresponds to your third of the wealth. If you were to leave today, she'd be prepared to pay you immediately with works of art and antiques."

Little by little, Broyz had begun to hate Fabio and this Dr Alves. He held them both secretly responsible for conspiring to keep him away from Fernanda. Who were they to forbid him from entering her bedroom? He would go there anyway, without anybody noticing. He would show them just what he was capable of.

He went down the spiral staircase on tiptoes. He cast an eye around the hall on the ground floor, that room dominated by the portrait of the deceased. Not one shadow moved. With assured steps, he reached the wide staircase that led to the second floor. Footsteps drew nearer, he froze. Two cleaning maids approached, chatting away quietly. He took a walk around the furniture, as though wandering distractedly. When the girls were out of sight, he took to the stairs with determination.

Dr Alves was just leaving Fernanda's bedroom. As their eyes met, Broyz raised his hands as if to say, "I give in, you've caught me," but Alves didn't seem worried by the husband's presence at the bedroom door. On the contrary, he smiled.

"Senhor Broyz," he said cheerfully, offering his hand, " it's a pleasure to see you after all this time. In fact, I wished to speak to you. I remember that conversation in the garden and I believe that …"

"How about if we talk inside?" interrupted Broyz, pointing to the bedroom.

The doctor shook his head and continued, taking no notice.

"Up until last week, I believed your wife had cholera. In fact, I discovered a small flea under her left armpit."

" A flea?" enquired Broyz, alarmed.

"We have to analyze the situation calmly. Many of the symptoms of African fever are identical to those of cholera, fleas for example …"

"Could we go inside and look at that flea together," proposed Broyz, not hiding his anxiety.

"There, in the bedroom?"

"You don't want me to see my wife, is that right, Dr Alves?" exclaimed Broyz, indignantly.

The doctor held up the palms of his hands, attempting to pacify Broyz.

"You're mistaken, you shouldn't think that. It's not me who forbids you to enter, but her."

"Her?" said Broyz in astonishment, and seized by sudden fury he launched himself against the door, which refused to accept defeat, suggesting a chair or piece of furniture blocked it from within. He focused the weight of his whole body behind one shoulder and flung himself at the door. It emitted a slight creak.

"Open, open right now!" he began to shout.

The handle turned, and through the tiniest of gaps, the shiny oval-shaped head of Fabio peered out, scrutinizing him severely. The servant's mouth, hidden beneath his large moustache, seemed to snarl as he uttered:

"Senhor Broyz, I'm warning you. You know you cannot come in. Anyway, the senhora is sleeping, she has a fever. It'd be unwise to wake her."

Broyz clenched his fists and, without saying a word, turned to look for Alves.

"Doctor?" he called. He intended proposing a joint visit to the university library, to consult the books and study a suitable treatment. He called after him once more as he rushed down the stairs, but Alves had already departed.

"And now they intend to place a light in our streets which is the same as sunlight, as though the day should never end," said

Friar Teresino in his Sunday sermon. "Will they also suggest we stop sleeping? A village without rest and without night is dangerous for mankind, above all for men of faith. My children, one has only to look at the insects attracted by the fire who kill themselves in its flames." The friar paused briefly before resuming. "Some day they will understand God did not create night for us to live in like bats."

As Dr Alves had preceded him and was the occupant of the guest-room at Mister Roger's home, Luís Agua had to rent a modest room at the notary's house.

He soon learnt the village abounded in secret, ancestral codes that were more prevalent than at first appeared. The architecture revealed a clear difference between the many poor houses and the few rich ones. In a way, it was the public face of the marked division between the peasants and artisans of the village, followers of the friar for the most part, and those others known as the "notables," among whom Mister Roger was prominent.

Agua's arrival, or the "arrival of progress," as the Englishman insisted on terming it, accentuated those divisions. At the periodic gatherings the notables organized away from the church, and to which Dr Alves, the notary and his nephew would occasionally attend, Mister Roger used two keen terms to differentiate between each group: those in favour of electricity were known as the "illuminatists", and those parishioners who supported the friar became the "obscurantists".

The "illuminatists" heaped praise on Agua at their meetings, as though he was the demiurge of everything they venerated. And, of everyone, it was the notary who paid him the most fulsome attention, determined as he was to combat the friar's preachings.

"You could help us," he told Agua one night.

"Me? In what way?"

"You come from a big city and you know their ways. You could tell the villagers that nowhere else do they fight progress, light and electricity as they are doing here."

"Being an outsider doesn't mean being neutral," replied Agua. "Everyone knows I'm an interested party. And while I speak in the name of my company, Friar Teresino has the advantage of speaking in the name of God."

"Nevertheless, there's one possibility ..." Mister Roger hinted, and then paused.

"Go on, please," the others asked.

"I was just thinking," continued the Englishman, "in this town there's something even bigger than the parish church, something that exerts almost the same sense of respect and fear over the villagers. I'm talking about the castle, of course ... If you were to install electricity in the castle, imagine it, a monument of lights, the cathedral of progress! Nobody could resist such a vision."

"There couldn't be a worse moment for that idea," the doctor interrupted. "What with the senhora's illness, I mean."

"That's true," conceded the Englishman. "If Fernanda were well, I'd convince her in a flash. However, there's no need to give up. It just means waiting. We'll convince her as soon as she recovers."

Some days later, Senhora Fernanda passed away in her sleep. Broyz had stepped out early for a walk in the park and on his return heard an unusual commotion on the top floor. He ran to the bedroom to find Fabio and two other servants trying to tip the body onto a stretcher. The bed looked different, as if a tornado had travelled through.

In the garden, balanced on a mound of dark wood, lay an open mahogany coffin, awaiting the stretcher with Fernanda's corpse to be brought down. The servants had formed an impromptu line, shoulder to shoulder. The widow's body arrived and was placed inside the coffin without sealing the lid. When Fabio was adjusting the dangling arms, crossing them over her belly, Broyz noticed Alma staring at him with tears in her eyes.

"*The two of us for ever.*"

Broyz couldn't prevent himself from dwelling on the inscription engraved on the tombstone. That inscription was now to become reality. He looked at the bare arms inside the coffin and noticed the widow was not wearing her bracelet. Aware that the other one, the twin bracelet, was already waiting at Antunes' mausoleum, he told himself it wouldn't be a bad idea to entomb Fernanda wearing her bracelet, and so he departed directly to fetch it.

He entered the bedroom where the great candelabra was still alight. If no servant had dared extinguish it, it was probably because the act of bothering with such a triviality could be misinterpreted in such circumstances as lack of sensitivity. He blew out the candles, leaving one flame as a mark of respect to Fernanda, and began to look for the bracelet in the chest of drawers, the bedside table, probing the cases, patting down the jumbled sheets. It took a while before he discovered it, discarded in a corner. And then he heard shouts from the park and the sound of horses' hooves. The cortege was leaving for the cemetery without him.

He ran in haste to the park and signalled vainly for the last carriage to stop. He'd suspected all along it was part of a plot to leave him behind deliberately, without carriage or horses.

He set off on foot, reaching the burial ground late, and had to tolerate being the target of whisperings. They were already throwing earth over the coffin. Friar Teresino had just pronounced the obligatory words and stood clasping an enormous cross against his belly, flanked by two altar boys carrying holy water. However, the servants not only whispered about his late arrival, but also discussed whether or not to return to the castle, whether to ignore or obey the new master's orders.

Broyz was equally uncertain, if not more so than them, and when the burial was over, instead of going to the castle, he walked to Vila Natal. He had promised to leave only if Fernanda recovered. What now? As he made his way towards his old house in the village, which he hadn't visited since his wedding, he imagined the servants had by now secured the doors, main gate and castle windows. He imagined they were ransacking it, carrying off all the possessions, both his and those belonging to the Antunes Coelho family.

Even though he longed to settle once more in his house in Rua Simões, he couldn't or mustn't leave everything to the mercy of the servants. Suddenly, he was struck by a thought: "The Castle doesn't belong to me!" He reproached himself immediately: "Fernanda would never forgive me for simply abandoning it!"

That night, more than ever, the village seemed like a labyrinth of narrow streets and squalid houses. He cut diagonally through the central square, continued walking along the main road, then turned west and skirted the row of identical façades until he reached his home. From behind the door, voices and laughter could be heard. He knocked once, twice ... twice again ... all his indignation concentrated in his fists. For a few seconds the unfamiliar voices fell silent. Then they launched into insulting him, little realizing he was the owner of the house in which they were squatting.

"Get out of there, or I'll have you ejected," he shouted.

Someone in the middle of a group of inhabitants gathered behind his back asked him sarcastically if it wasn't enough to be the new owner of the castle.

"This house belonged to my father and is now mine," he replied.

It wasn't in Broyz's character to offer explanations to strangers, but the situation seemed to necessitate it.

"And why do you want the house?" insisted one of the crowd. "Isn't the inheritance enough?"

Broyz thought he recognized a few faces addressing him: former employees of his father, some people who had treated him kindly during his childhood. Now these self-same people showed him their antipathy. To hell with them, he thought. He would try and recover his house in more favourable circumstances. He turned his back on the crowd and their gossiping. "You should be ashamed, the senhora died this very day and you're already here," he caught from one side. Head hung low, and with the gait of someone who had lost too much in one single day, Broyz made his way back towards the castle.

59

CHAPTER FIVE

THE SERVANTS continued to flee and Broyz cursed every morning when they assembled in the kitchen and the count revealed one or two less than the night before, three less than the night preceding that, ten less than a week earlier. Out of the thirty or more who had welcomed him that afternoon when Fernanda proposed the wedding arrangement, only nine remained. Worse still, the youngest and healthiest had departed at the first opportunity. Further flights had followed after Broyz had cautiously communicated through Fabio that he was considering retaining the total profit from the harvest of the adjoining lands, embracing the authority as conferred by the will.

Aside from the flight of these servants, the last days of 1921 passed off uneventfully. Broyz resolved not to leave his room at the top of the tower, revealing that his outlook remained one of trepidation. What is the tower of a castle after all, if not the furthermost point of defence? Something had improved, however: Alma no longer felt obliged to prepare his meals for this in secret.

One morning, Broyz attempted to take down the large portrait of Antunes Coelho presiding over the hall and shift it to the room known as the study. None of the servants wanted to help. Each argued one excuse or another: the frame was stuck to the wall; it was too heavy; being fragile it could be damaged in transit; and, finally, access to the study was forbidden.

He determined to move it alone. The portrait was very heavy, as though Antunes in person. When Broyz reached the study, he found the door locked.

"Fabio!" he called, and asked for the key.

"The key?" replied Fabio. "I've never had it, senhor."

"Someone must have it …"

"I don't know who, senhor."

Broyz had certainly seen that key in the hands of another servant, Hélio, the same fellow whose job it was to bring milk and food for the cat. Yet that man had been one of the first to take flight and now, no matter how much Broyz suspected the key was in Fabio's hands, he had no means of proving it.

"Okay," he said, without losing his calm. He was confronting the servant for the first time and thought he'd found the right tone between strict and fatuous. "In that case, Fabio," he ordered. "We'll have to knock it down."

The old servant shook his head, as though lamenting Broyz's suggestion.

"Didn't you hear me? Knock it down. It's not my order, it comes from the Senhora and Senhor Antunes."

"Is that so?" Fabio mocked.

"That's right. Do you want to be held responsible if the senhor's cat dies of hunger?"

"The cat!" Fabio exclaimed.

Broyz couldn't ascertain if that cry meant Fabio was genuinely unaware of the key's whereabouts or if mention of the cat had served to uproot his disobedience.

His doubts increased when the door was forced and they found no trace of the animal inside.

Broyz took the portrait of Antunes and leaned it against a wall. Then he noticed another painting quite alike in terms of its technique and colours. Who was the man? He hesitated a moment before recognizing him: Captain Acevedo, although a good deal younger, perhaps twenty or even thirty years earlier. Another object caught his attention, a notebook, or so it seemed, that turned out to be an album, a detailed scrapbook of newspaper cuttings, its pages filled with aeroplanes and aviators such as the Wright Brothers, Henri Farman or Alberto Santos-Dumont. Some news items, highlighted in ink, stood out from the rest: The Frenchman, Louis Blériot, has made the first Channel crossing, read one headline from July 1909. The newspapers of the day also referred to the cyclist Paul Cornu, inventor of the earliest helicopter, to intrepid and pioneering parachutists and to a North American troupe of aerial jugglers who climbed onto the wings of small aeroplanes or atop air balloons in mid-flight. Broyz pondered the meaning of these cuttings and the painting as he stepped from the study. Outside the servants were holding a lively discussion.

"Would Hélio have taken the cat?"

"Perhaps it escaped through Hélio's negligence and is now roaming the park."

"Perhaps the dogs have already killed it."

The servants were still debating the whereabouts of the animal when Fabio clapped his hands and called for silence.

"We must search for him in the park. You too," he said, pointing at Broyz. "You must help too."

"Me? Yes, of course," Broyz answered obligingly, though he knew immediately that he would never be able to tell the cat apart from the others that tended to wander through the park, simply because he'd never seen it before.

The search lasted almost two days. They divided into three groups, and each returned at dusk on the second day with a cat that didn't belong to Antunes. His cat was domestic, old and sickly. These were stray, wild and fearless before dogs. Side by side, the three bore no resemblance to one another, not in the slightest. One cat was fat and jet black, another white, that walked with a crestfallen amble, and a third coffee and white, with big eyes and a curious triangular marking between the ears. Eventually, after admitting to Broyz they had never paid attention to the physiognomy of the creature that depended upon Hélio's kindness, the servants acknowledged defeat. Monotony and routine returned to the castle, only interrupted many days later by a fresh visit from the doctor.

"I'm sorry to bring bad tidings," said Alves to Broyz. "What killed the senhora could indeed have been African fever."

"How do you know?"

"There've been other cases in the region. It seems we're dealing with an epidemic that extends as far as Coimbra, although nothing is proven. There's one way to check."

"And that is?"

"It might strike you as unpleasant," Alves warned. "But, to confirm our suspicions, we must exhume the corpse and examine it thoroughly."

"I don't know. It's dangerous," replied Broyz. "We could all become infected. And, it's forbidden. If Friar Teresino found out, we'd never hear the end of it."

"Think it over calmly," Alves said, smiling.

The following night was not the most propitious for trespassing beyond the cemetery gate. There were no clouds, unlike recent times, and the full moon bathed the tombstones with its pearly light.

It had been Alves' idea to solicit the services of two men who could dig with speed and precision.

"Well?" Broyz asked the doctor after almost two hours of examination.

"I've my doubts: these could be indications of cholera, but also typhus ... There's something peculiar about the way in which the symptoms have combined," said Alves.

"This means Fernanda had contracted African fever," Broyz concluded somewhat hastily.

The doctor shrugged his shoulders and instructed the men to return the coffin to the ground. Back at the castle, Broyz wanted to know what measures Alves would take in case of an epidemic.

"Doctor Xavier, you're the only doctor in Vila Natal, and back there in the cemetery I overheard you order the coffin to be buried at a depth of five metres, didn't I?"

"Yes, I did say that," Alves replied, little appreciating why Broyz was taking such a circuitous route.

"I mean, doctor, you and I studied in the same classrooms and read the same books ..." Broyz coughed and cleared his throat. "I know you gave instructions for the coffin to be buried at such a depth to prevent contagious vapours from reaching the surface. That's what the best books recommend. And the second recommendation is that each person suspected of being infectious should be locked in, his house boarded, his door marked with a red cross, and all the occupants quarantined."

"I understand your anguish, Senhor Broyz, but you mustn't ..."

"Let me tell you something," Broyz interrupted. "It's too late now for all that. Most of the servants have fled the castle, the risks of contagion have been multiplied already."

"I know … but you're mistaken about one thing: I'm not the only doctor in the village."

"Ah, no," protested Broyz, noticing Alves pointing his finger at him. "Never mind that I finished my studies, I'm not going to dedicate myself to looking after the sick."

"I'll be blunt," said Alves, "this epidemic may flare up in a matter of weeks … I know I'm going to need your help, and if you're prepared to collaborate, I could overlook your quarantine. You see, Broyz, it's not just my idea …"

"I don't understand."

"I must go now," Alves apologized, "but read this letter and you'll understand."

In short, the letter said that after all the help the University had given by sending Dr Alves to attend to Fernanda, it was now his turn to return the favour.

"Dr Alves will explain to you in person about an exotic disease that seems in some respects to be like cholera, but also shares the characteristics of African fevers. If the threat of an epidemic is confirmed, the doctors will be unable to cope. I'm sorry to say Vila Natal has no doctors other than Alves and yourself. As we are aware that you never collected your diploma, we are enclosing documents that will serve as provisional registration,"

the letter said. And continued:

"As regards that pamphlet about buttocks that some practical joker signed in your name, we regret to inform you that it continues to be distributed behind our backs among the students. Even more serious is the fact that this same joker had another pamphlet printed a few weeks ago with an even more obscene text that we have decided not to send for reasons of decency. Rest assured, Senhor Broyz, we are tracking down the perpetrator; and it would be of great help to us if you could convey any suspicions pertaining to the matter. Do you remember, for example, any former colleague with whom you had a particular rivalry?"

Broyz paused, placed the letter to one side and cast his mind back: anatomy, pharmacy, hygiene, chemistry, botany, physiology … there were so many subjects, each in turn corresponding to hundreds of pupils, faces and names, that he could barely remember the dozens of occasional acquaintances and as many rivals, also occasional, because he was not the type to make lasting enemies.

"*If you have any suspicions, do not hesitate to let us know*," the letter concluded.

Then came the rector's signature, which was not his usual signature. This concerned Broyz as much as the contents he'd just finished reading. Death had taken away old Jardim de Vilhena at a bad moment, the former rector would have already discovered the practical joker responsible for the catalogue. Instead, his replacement, named Souto, had now to investigate the matter from scratch.

Broyz didn't manage to fall asleep at once. The moon was high, the dogs barked louder than usual, and when he did eventually fall asleep, he had a terrible dream.

In Broyz' dream, Fabio was trying to escape from the castle and two men, the same ones whom Alves had engaged to dig up the burial ground, were lighting torches and pursuing him with the dogs.

In Broyz's dream, Fabio heard the first sounds of barking and ran through the main gate and headed for the beach, covering his ears because the barking was getting closer and was beginning to bewilder him, and the men were tiring before the dogs, now straining at the leashes, and their hands and feet were painful and they stumbled, and the dogs had broken free and were practically clawing into Fabio who kept running, and crashed into a bush, falling to the ground where the dogs pounced with frothing jaws and Fabio's sweat turned to blood and mingled with the earth.

In Broyz's dream, the dogs returned slowly to the castle, found the exhausted men half-way along the route, came up wagging their tails and licking the men's faces tenderly, covering them with blood, their panting and drooling tongues stained red as never before, letting Fabio's short-lived freedom flutter like a flag.

Awaking from his nightmare, Broyz opened one eye and thought he made out the somewhat hunched back of Fabio vaguely outlined in the early morning sun filtering through the curtains. He was quietly reading the rector's letter, careful not to touch the paper, lest the slightest sound should betray his presence.

Fabio survived the dream, thought Broyz. He considered shouting something, reprimanding him for his curiosity and insolence, but he was too exhausted and couldn't summon up his voice from the depths of his throat. In any case, it was too late now for any sort of reaction, even if he were to challenge Fabio it wouldn't stop the rumours spreading about the epidemic.

Broyz swiftly closed his eyes, pretending to be still asleep, before the servant could turn to face the bed. As a matter of fact, he had the impression he'd fallen asleep for when he reopened his eyes—how much later?—the light entering the room was different, more resplendent, and the servant's behaviour waking Broyz, likewise, seemed even more audacious and intrusive, a task Fabio undertook without even being asked.

Was the letter still there? Yes, there it was on the table, although Fabio avoided it so naturally Broyz hesitated. What if, perhaps, as with the dogs, he had also dreamt of his back? Yet, if that feverish pursuit had without doubt been a dream, the presence of Fabio spying in his room, on the other hand, was too realistic to have been an hallucination. Fabio had shown himself capable of such behaviour and more, to the extent he wouldn't hesitate in banging the mattress and giving Broyz gentle shoves to force him out of bed.

Shaking off sleep, Broyz went downstairs, ready for his walk in the park. On reaching the foot of the battlement tower, he noticed the dogs. His attention had already been drawn to the air of stillness that prevailed, a stillness unimaginable at that hour when the servants were usually bustling about and the dogs barking ceaselessly. He understood the silence. The dogs lay on the lawn, some dead, others ill or in their death throes, struck down by the epidemic, their muzzles paralyzed, their eyes bulging from sockets, their paws splayed apart. What seemed to have befallen all the characters of his dream was most strange. As if by dreaming them, he'd cast a spell on them. The dogs had died or fallen ill. Fabio looked troubled, as if carrying an inexplicable weight upon his shoulders. And stillness had risen all around the place.

Despite the stench emanating from the infected animals, the day was so bright Broyz decided to extend his walk to include the stables. For the same reason as the dogs, the horses had laid down and refused to eat any food. Broyz was more concerned, however, for the dogs, stretched out there at the foot of the tower in the hot sun. Alves had told him that if the epidemic began claiming new victims, he must bury them straight away, bury them deep.

It crossed his mind to call the servants and order the burial of the dead animals. Nobody responded to his calls. He shouted again, to no avail. The stillness seemed to intensify. Just then, he spotted the figure of Alma approaching unhurriedly, and he ran to intercept and protect her from the sight of the dogs.

"Where's everyone?" Broyz asked.

She informed him the last of the servants, including Fabio, had fled a few minutes before.

Broyz calculated that Alma was unable to see the animals from where she stood, which was just as well, because she shouldn't know about the epidemic, unless she had already heard from Fabio. Of course, if that was the case, if Alma knew, Broyz valued her all the more for staying behind.

He asked Alma to return to the kitchen and prepare lunch. Meanwhile, he set about burying the dogs, a task that required more than an hour's work. After burying the dead, he then paused to contemplate those on the verge of dying, their hours numbered, their destiny inescapable. He determined to administer mercy in the form of a blow to the skull and bury them directly. Back at the castle, he suggested to Alma she serve lunch at the table in the hall, until then only employed to display an empty vase. She agreed, smiling, and spread the table-cloth that nobody had removed from the chest since the death of

Senhor Antunes. Broyz's attitude, however, was thoroughly surprising to her; instead of being angry, or preoccupied with the latest flights, he seemed in good humour.

So unusual was his behaviour he didn't even seem bothered that the last of the servants had looted the cellars, making off with their provisions.

"How will we live without money or food?" asked Alma. Her question went unanswered. They finished lunch and Broyz fell onto the sofa and stretched out his legs fully. It was as if his body was releasing all the pressures of the last few days. For the first time he enjoyed complete freedom, away from the prying eyes of servants; for the first time he felt the castle was his, an idea that neither distressed nor inconvenienced him. When he awoke, Alma was nowhere to be seen, though the sound of her footsteps on the floor above were just audible, like the drips of a liquid falling on soil. Broyz could hear a dance of footsteps, drawing away and then coming back, rising then falling, faster then slower. Alma's feet no longer needed to keep to the same paths as before, when she was one servant among many. Now they could savour flights of fancy.

"Alma!" Broyz called, and she replied she would be down just as soon as she'd finished tidying. He called again, this time solely for the pleasure of uttering her name and listening for the echo.

When she came down, it had grown dark. She sat next to Broyz, clasped her hands around her knees and without further ado began to recount the story of her life. She had been born there eighteen years ago; her mother having worked as a chamber-maid in the castle, until she died, without revealing her father's name. For a long time, she'd suspected Senhor Antunes was her father, not only because certain features, her chin, the shape of her eyes and the curve of her lips, were similar, but also because of the exaggerated affection Antunes showed towards her during her childhood. In other words, the senhor had raised Alma to become his maidservant. Broyz was fascinated by this turn in the story and was eager to hear the rest. Alma spoke of her mother's Spanish origins, uttering two or three phrases in that language as if proof. By this point, Broyz's only thought was that the young girl was probably a worthier heiress to the castle than him.

Alma finished her tale and made herself comfortable, copying his position, avoiding her feet touching the floor. The sofa seemed a safe island, surrounded by silence, where they were both shipwrecked. Even as Alma avoided contact with the floor, her dress, hair and forearms unintentionally caressed him. However much Broyz was excited by these slight brushings against him, he remained in his place, and in this respect, Alma thought he was different from other masters she had known or that other maidservants had described. During their time alone, he'd never tried to take advantage of her; he didn't presume rights to possess her just because he gave the orders and she was the servant. Undoubtedly, he desired her, she thought, just from the way his eyes lingered on her lips or her neckline, but his wasn't a violent desire.

Darkness slowly invaded the sofa and they lit candles to climb the stairs, each with their own candlestick, Alma's held level with her eyes. When they reached the landing, a draught extinguished Alma's. She stumbled and the candlestick rolled away down the stairs. Broyz grasped her with his free hand and guided her up the last flight, at which point there was no call to bid each other goodnight.

"I've heard rumours that some people are trying to twist my words," said Friar Teresino in his Sunday sermon. "When I speak out against artificial lighting, I'm not advocating darkness, as the defenders of such outlandish inventions maintain. All of you, my children, are aware of the immense and peaceful darkness that surrounds us when we shut our eyes as a sign of devotion. It's a wave of peace, a journey to the depths of our purity, to our innermost sanctity. Of course, I don't want to promote the darkness of evil. Yet, neither do I mean that the shadows of Satan should be illuminated with fireworks. If you've seen fireworks, you'll understand what I mean. What remains in the night sky and in our spirit when the flares have extinguished? What of the din and the feast? Let's return, my children, to a state of harmony and simplicity. Let's live, then, enriched by the light of God."

Friar Emilio turned to Luís Agua with a quiet smile and said:

"We're very satisfied with the progress of the work."

Although Agua didn't have much sympathy with the clergy, he particularly liked this friar. Of course, he didn't share all his views, but he admired his courage in coping with the plague and his devotion towards his sick patients. Since his last visit to the monastery, he still hadn't managed to erase the memory of the voices of those dying. Again and again that plaintive choir returned to haunt him, and in private conversations with Dr Alves his worst fears concerning the epidemic were confirmed. Nevertheless, he maintained the absurd hope the friar would tell him, on this visit, that he no longer housed the sick, and that the plague was transitory.

"Friar Emilio, how is everything going down there?" he eventually ventured to ask, without mentioning the word plague.

"Worse each day, my son," replied the friar. He paused, then added: "Worst of all is the intolerable heat sent by the devil."

Agua considered it an opportune moment to offer some friendly advice, and he recommended Dr Alves as an expert in African fever. "I'll tell him myself to come and help," said Agua, before leaving the monastery for Pombal, where he stopped for only a few hours, there being little he could do without his demonstration equipment, still awaiting removal from Coimbra. He promised to return as soon as he regained it. Vila Natal was his next destination; he was eager to return as he'd grown fond of the village. Only the problem of his lodgings required resolution. He could no longer endure being a guest in the notary's house, not because the small room he rented was in bad shape, but because the notary and his nephew did not inspire him with confidence. There had been some arguments during the past week, disputes that made living together uncomfortable.

As Dr Alves still lodged with Mister Roger, Agua decided to ask to stay at the home of a wealthy carpet-maker called Amaral, a recommendation by the Englishman himself. Viewed from outside, Paulo Amaral's house, where a loom also operated, was impeccable, divided by eight windows, one corresponding to Agua's new room. Viewed from inside, on the other hand, the house showed signs of neglect and cried out for numerous repairs. Nevertheless, even though the beams could be seen through the crumbling ceiling, even though the wallpapering was a disaster, even though the heating had been ripped from its fixtures, and the only candle barely emitted any light from its pathetic flame, Luís Agua preferred all this, alongside the tranquility of Amaral and his wife, to the tactless remarks of the notary and his nephew.

He had been settled for some time when one of the altar boys came in search of him to say that Friar Teresino invited him to the church that same afternoon for a talk. Surprised, Agua didn't know what excuse to invent to avoid the long sermon that, as far as he could judge, awaited him. He could always snub the friar and invent any excuse at a later date. Yet, the prospect of such a meeting intrigued him, and shortly afterwards, rising from the depths of his mind, two voices, one just like his own, the other imitating the friar, began to initiate a conversation about progress and electricity, the friar's voice being the most predominant.

"Have you read Gogol?" A commanding voice quoted from memory a line from Gogol against "artificial light." A wavering voice replied that Gogol, if he remembered correctly, started as a writer and ended a mystic. The time for the meeting approached and the conversation in Agua's head continued to develop without any signs of a conclusion.

He went out towards the parish church, but the voices persisted. "What's happening?" thought a third voice, quite similar to the wavering one, but with the difference that Agua could silence it or make it speak at will. "What's happening to me?" Agua was completing his fifth circuit of the Praça da Estrela before the church when the imposing voice drew the conversation to an end. Prepared, he crossed the square to enter the church, convinced the scene that had just occurred in his head had been prophetic. Contrary to expectations, Friar Teresino welcomed him with a smile and showered him with compliments and questions: how was he enjoying his stay?—how was he getting along with the villagers?—how did he find the village?—where had he chosen to stay?

Agua started to feel considerably more at ease when the friar, still smiling, said to him point blank:

"Senhor Agua, I've called you here because I've a confession to make that cannot be postponed."

"Go ahead. You listen to so many every day it's about time the favour was returned."

"You're very kind," the friar exclaimed, ignoring Agua's cynicism. "Almost all atheists tend to be kind."

Silence. Friar Teresino wiped a handkerchief across his sweating bald patch and continued.

"Of course, you're asking yourself what is my confession. Well, no, it doesn't have to do with any sin. It so happens I've been re-thinking my ideas. You think I'm a dim-witted friar, isn't that so, Senhor Agua?"

"I only think you despise electricity with an inexplicable fanaticism."

Friar Teresino looked him in the eyes. Never before had anyone spoken to him in such a frank manner, let alone in the surroundings of his own office. Should he demand more respect? Or had he encouraged such confidence by treating him so casually as an atheist? He told himself it wasn't a matter of pride and continued talking, regardless. Judging from Agua's expression, it was obvious he was eagerly awaiting the confession. The confession, of course! He had even rehearsed it that same morning!

Everything the friar had to say can be summed up in a few words. It was not that generically termed electricity he wished to oppose from the pulpit, but something far more precise: electric light.

"Electric light?" repeated Agua.

The problem with the lamplight in the streets, and in this case Agua recognized it as a somewhat polemical issue, was that a new public space had been created beneath the lamp posts. The illuminated streets shed light on everything that had remained shadowy until then: poverty and madness, crime and bohemia, lies and prostitution ... something of the sort had occurred in Paris around 1860, and the time of the inauguration of Napoleon III's grand boulevards. With electricity, much more than with the old gas street lamps, everything that had traditionally been mysterious had become pure presence. The fact Agua understood didn't mean he shared the idea of throwing a mantle of semi-darkness over everything unpleasant. Did Friar Teresino really believe sin flourished beneath the lamplight? Of course he did. And he wasn't alone in his belief either. A writer that Teresino read devotedly had written on the subject. "*The devil himself ignites the lamps so that everything shines beneath an unnatural light*," he declaimed, as though he was in the pulpit.

"Gogol," exclaimed Agua.

The friar opened wide his arms and raised them towards heaven.

"You know Gogol? You know him? Isn't he wonderful?"

Agua shivered and said nothing.

"Look, Senhor Agua, behind the church are some large huts," yes, Agua had seen them, "that I've decided to refurbish. You must know that symptoms of an epidemic have become manifest among the peasants," yes, Agua knew, "obliging many to seek refuge here, near God and medicine. This misfortune certainly made me rethink that offer of yours. Don't get me wrong ..." no, Agua wasn't getting him wrong, "I don't wish to lavish lights upon my church façade in times of sickness. I only wish to light up the inside of the large huts to provide shelter for the infected."

The large huts? Disappointedly, Agua reflected the work envisaged by the friar was of little use to his promotional ends. It distressed him that in the nearby towns such as Fátima or Leiria, the religious authorities showed more enthusiasm. The smaller the village, the more conservative the parish seemed. Nevertheless, how could he now refuse to work for Friar Teresino? To refuse was tantamount to asking for excommunication, exposing himself to the possibility the friar's fury might reach Lisbon, perhaps even the ears of his own bosses. To agree, on the other hand, was the first convenient step towards the necessary blessing for "unnatural light."

"If you could ensure me the help of half a dozen followers, I could begin work in two weeks."

"Wonderful," said the friar. "May God bless you, God bless you!"

One month later, on the 23rd of January 1922, the first letter arrived. It bore the signature of a certain Tomás Antunes Coelho, who claimed to be a relative of the deceased Antunes and who purported to reside in Coimbra. More importantly, this Tomás was reclaiming the inheritance of the castle and its possessions. The validity of the will was in doubt. If the Antunes Coelho dynasty had not disappeared following Fernanda's death, then this Tomás was the rightful heir instead of Broyz.

The first letter was vague beyond belief: this Tomás didn't indicate what the nature of his relationship was, or where he could be contacted (it was hardly enough to say inhabitant of Coimbra). Neither did he specify what legal measures he would take, nor announce any visit to the castle, all of which would have at least been logical. In actual fact, this relation seemed more dedicated to intimidating and making his presence felt than recovering the family riches. And when further letters followed, Broyz ran up against the same threats, culminating neither in a concrete plan nor a conciliatory proposal. This Tomás didn't state, "you must leave the castle," but rather, "you should leave …", he didn't say, "I'm entitled to," but rather, "I suppose I should be entitled to …" Nor did he mention the name of a lawyer with whom Broyz could make contact.

What intrigued Broyz most was how the letters managed to

arrive. Perhaps a messenger, a traveller or a postal worker slipped them into the precarious letterbox to one side of the entrance gate. Alma had discovered the first by chance. All the subsequent letters also appeared in the box, yet the postmarks on their stamps were so worn as to prevent Broyz from confirming if indeed the envelopes were posted in Coimbra.

The unforeseen appearance of this Tomás complicated everything. Both Broyz and Alma had thought to spend a carefree few months selling the oldest works of art. In the meantime, they would consider the eventuality of selling the castle and moving to Coimbra with a tidy sum of money. Now the inheritance was in doubt, Broyz could no longer do as he pleased with the building and all the objects within. What would happen if this Tomás annulled the deceased's will? Would Broyz have to pay him back the money from the sale of everything?

The solution, Alma pointed out, was Mister Roger. Only the Englishman would know how to keep a secret, buying various pieces, in particular those loosely inventorized in the will, and selling them abroad, where this Tomás would never be able to find out. There were a number of unsettled matters between Broyz and Mister Roger, but there was nothing better than a business deal to bridge that distance, and so Broyz sent Alma with a bundle of antiques to try to obtain the best possible price from the Englishman. At the express orders of Dr Alves, Broyz was not allowed to leave the castle, and thus Alma mounted a sickly horse and departed for Vila Natal.

Mister Roger received her with distrust and, noticing the valuable objects, took her for a thief, one of the many servants who had fled the castle. Nevertheless, the objects were so tempting he decided to buy them.

With the money received, not a great deal, Alma purchased two sacks of food. On her return, Broyz sensed her anxiety. "The horse died halfway home," she said, stumbling over her words, so much was there to tell, so much had she seen and heard in the streets and parish of Vila Natal, where there were already dozens of sick people.

Broyz feigned surprise at the news, as though he'd never heard about the epidemic, while, in reality, the wave of contagion preoccupied him as much, if not more, in recent times than the matter of the letters. The difference between both preoccupations was with the epidemic everything seemed explicit and irrevocable, while the correspondence from Coimbra was trying his patience: did Tomás Antunes Coelho exist, or was he the creation of someone envious? And if he rejected the true existence of this Tomás, who then was the instigator of those letters?

Could it be Fabio, or some other servant, whose sole intention was to harass them and prevent them from leading a quiet life in the castle now that both remained there alone? At this point, Broyz knew that those servants who had fled were spreading all sorts of rumours in the village about Alma staying at his side. Nevertheless, he couldn't imagine the servants, who hardly knew how to write, conspiring around a feather pen and inkwell.

Could it be, perhaps, the same person responsible for the catalogue of bottoms? There was something of a resemblance between the script of that catalogue and the numerous paragraphs from the supposed relative. In that case, this Tomás had perhaps studied medicine, like him. In contrast to the characteristic seriousness among law students, there was a *Livro dos Quartanistas da Medicina* circulating in Coimbra, a satirical work full of obscene comments and caricatures, typical of the leg-pulling attitude that existed in the faculty. And though Broyz didn't remember any colleague called Antunes Coelho, he did vaguely remember a Antonio Pires who couldn't live without playing jokes, and who never ceased trying to shock students with fingers or eyes snatched from corpses and slipped, surreptitiously, into the pockets of their white coats.

Yet, even supposing this Antonio Pires had written the catalogue of bottoms, even supposing he'd adopted the alias of Tomás Antunes Coelho to feed his joker's spirit, Broyz wondered how Pires, or any other former student colleague, could have found out everything about the will and inheritance of the castle, or his marriage to the widow and her death. Someone living so far away could not possibly acquire so many details.

In Vila Natal everyone knew about everything, as usual in a small village, but Coimbra was a big city, away from all that particular gossip.

And what about Alves? Broyz liked Dr Alves more and more. All the same, what if he wasn't the honest man he seemed? What if it was his ambition to take possession of the castle and its treasures? It was clearly the case that Alves could've evicted him by arguing that an epidemic was breaking out, that the castle constituted a centre of infection and the prophylaxis obliged a measure of that kind. Nevertheless, he hadn't done that. How could he doubt him? Broyz reproached himself.

There were still further suspects, although less likely. Captain Acevedo? Broyz knew he was somewhere abroad. Friar Teresino? Impossible. Mister Roger? It was true Broyz had seen him in a bad light since his father's death, but the Englishman was too busy with other forms of strategy; a man of the world, a shrewd businessman like him, an art lover, such a person would not send threatening, almost insulting letters, without any sort of explanation.

Such thoughts were preoccupying Broyz when Mister Roger turned up at the castle. His presence seemed to counteract Broyz's sneaking suspicions. However, the reason for his visit, he said, was that he had decided to return to London.

"To London? When?" asked Broyz earnestly.

"In a matter of weeks, after tying up a few matters."

"I don't know how we'll manage to obtain money and food now, but let me congratulate you."

Mister Roger's eyes opened wide. Was Broyz genuinely glad he was leaving or did he have another purpose?

"Of course I congratulate you," explained Broyz, "because the epidemic will soon overtake the village." He spoke quietly, almost in a whisper so that Alma wouldn't hear the word epidemic from the kitchen.

The old man seemed exhausted, with his sagging cheeks and sweating brow; his skin had become ochre-coloured.

"As you know, Dr Alves is at my house. If you've any problem, don't hesitate to call on him."

"It's not Mister Roger who's writing the letters," noted Broyz as soon as the Englishman had left.

Alma, who, until then, had endured the endless surmising, glared angrily at him.

"That's enough, please," she exclaimed. "Why do you persist in thinking Tomás Antunes Coelho doesn't exist? Surely it's simpler to accept he does?"

"Of course it is," he replied. But it was precisely this simplicity that confirmed his non-existence.

Immediately afterwards, with the arrival of the seventh letter, Broyz thought he'd discovered messages reading between the lines he hadn't noticed before. Over three days he tried various approaches to see if he could come up with the hidden key. When the eighth arrived at the castle, he was truly exasperated by the game. Nothing threw any light upon the real identity of the sender.

CHAPTER SIX

URING one of the many "illuminatist" meetings, the notary and his nephew accused Agua of collusion with Friar Teresino. In their opinion, the friar's crusade against electricity concealed motives that had nothing to do with religion. As with many other villages, Vila Natal had recently dedicated itself to the manufacture of alcohol, and Friar Teresino himself supervised the production of a liquor that was fairly similar to sloe brandy, though less flavoured with aniseed and without cinnamon traces. The relative success of the friar's liquor had initiated a rivalry between the parish and the vine growers. With the arrival of electricity, Friar Teresino feared the industrialization of the grape harvest would threaten the sales of his liquor.

Mister Roger and others immediately came to the defence of Agua, stating he was unaware of these matters, but the notary continued his onslaught and shouted:

"How many sets of electrical equipment do you have?"

"Here … only one …" Agua stuttered, "but there's another on the way."

"It's obvious the friar has contracted your services to neutralize your equipment, to keep it under his control in the parish."

"Perhaps … perhaps," Mister Roger reflected aloud, directing a protective look at Agua.

"But the other set is about to arrive and, if you want, I can even ask for a third from Lisbon," said Agua.

"Well then, hurry up," suggested the notary, "soon, when the epidemic takes a real hold, they'll block off this region, isn't that right, doctor?"

"It's an open secret," said Alves. "We believe the initial demarcation zone will encompass Vila Natal, Leiria, Caminhos and Pombal, perhaps Coimbra too later. It'll be possible to circulate within the zone, but it'll be impossible to enter or leave. I advise you to write Lisbon straightaway if you want another set."

When, in mid-March, it emerged the government would indeed seal off the whole central region, a night convoy was hastily arranged to take Mister Roger, the notary and anyone else who wanted to depart, out of the zone towards Galicia. Although in support of this escape, Alves quickly realized that, without those two, the "illuminatists" would not only be reduced in numbers, but the balance of power between his group and the "obscurantists" would be shattered, something slightly worrying in a village where there had never been, not even in the era of the monarchy or the short lived republic of the 1910s, an appointed mayor.

Unexpectedly, the convoy departed with no other passengers than the notary and the Englishman. The peasants were afraid to abandon their lands; the craftsmen, their meagre belongings. As for the notables, not all fully appreciated the magnitude of the epidemic, especially as Alves only admitted in private, and then only to the people he trusted, the demoralizing prognoses circulating in Coimbra, and which was being curtailed in order not to increase the panic.

Being a doctor, Alves stayed on for obvious reasons, but he failed to understand the reasoning of those who, even when warned, remained. With some effort, he could explain away the passivity of the Amarals, rationalizing they were elderly, sedentary and bored by everything, but he was unable to justify Agua's decision, which he considered an act of suicide.

Urged to flee by Alves, Agua calmly told him he didn't intend leaving the village until his trunks had arrived from Coimbra. Arrival was imminent in his view. Besides, without his possessions, he was nobody. And being effectively nobody, he would stay there without further reflection.

"You're going to stay? Are you being serious?"

Agua wasn't joking, even if his reasons amounted to no more than inconsistent, truncated sentences that he completed with gestures.

He was waiting for his trunks … Mister Roger had left him in charge … the castle would look fantastic fully lit … he must convince the others to start work on the Avenue of Light … he had to convince Broyz to agree to electricity … and as the trunks were taking such a long time … the epidemic was not so serious … now he'd finished settling in … and as the friar was taking such a long time to invite him around again … should he name it, Avenue of Light, in the singular, or would it be better to use the plural, Avenue of Lights?

At the end of March, the military blocked the roads, marking out the restricted area. A little later, Friar Teresino interrupted work at the huts, arguing that the number of sick patients was growing continually, demanding all his energy. As soon as Agua learnt of this development, he requested a meeting with the friar to ask for the return of his equipment, though according to the altar boys who barely welcomed him, the friar was not available to receive him. "Come back in a few days time, please."

A few weeks later in May, the front line was moved forward a few kilometres to include the city of Coimbra within the prohibited zone. This measure made it possible for Agua's three trunks to reach him at last.

"You've made a serious mistake staying here," said Dr Alves. "What use are the trunks now when you're imprisoned in a restricted zone?"

"I don't know …" admitted Agua. "I don't know what I've done, it's as if I was asleep."

"Don't regret it now, my friend, think of a way out … think!"

At the end of June, Broyz fell ill. Alma made him stay in bed until the fever passed, though as soon as her attention was turned, Broyz rose and rushed to the tower window, from where he could survey the park with the help of a small pair of binoculars he'd found in the display cabinet in the main hall. Broyz hoped these binoculars would enable him to catch the messenger leaving the letters. In the meantime, he also spied other things from the tower: the castle surroundings; the nearby village; the start of the track that led to the river path; Alma's walks in the park; Alma's visits and attention to the one horse still alive; the late arrival of Dr Alves.

Although Alves had promised to visit him assiduously, it had been weeks since he last came, and this, Broyz thought, was most odd, given the doctor meant to check he never ventured beyond the castle's walls and obeyed the rector's instructions.

At the beginning, the fever climbed at night and fell at dawn, like a tide. Then, over a couple of nights, it failed to come down. Seized by fear and hallucinations, in a voice so deep it didn't seem like his own, Broyz spoke to Alma about the epidemic that came from afar, "creeping," he said, "like a monster." She replied it was impossible for in the castle they were safe from any catastrophe. Nevertheless, deep down, she feared the worst.

It wasn't long before the fever died away. And as soon as his cheeks regained some colour, Broyz wanted to know if the doctor had been round to examine him.

"Yes," she lied to calm him, saying that, according to Alves, his condition was not serious. Three weeks later, however, following the arrival of a letter from the notary demanding "the immediate presence of Senhor Broyz in my office," Alma deeply regretted having invented it all.

"I'm going to town," said Broyz one morning, and he prepared a travelling bag in which he placed some fairly valuable objects among his clothes.

"Suppose I take the opportunity to sell these relics? We've already spent the last of the money and finished nearly all the food."

Alma said nothing.

"By now," he continued, "I guess Mister Roger will have arrived in England. I pray his departure has been delayed. In which case, I'll ask the notary or Dr Alves to recommend a discreet buyer."

Alma wished him luck and begged him to take good care during the journey.

"Come on, woman, it's nothing. Not if the doctor said my health is not at risk!"

The ban on leaving the castle, a ban Alma was unaware of, counted for little, given the plague had spread to the village,

Broyz told himself. Thus convinced, he went in search of the last horse, which he found quite weak. The situation posed a dilemma: if he rode to the village, it was more than likely the poor animal would be overwhelmed by the effort; if he went on foot, he was placing an excessive risk on his health. He determined to ride by night, and half-way along the road, as anticipated, the horse began whinnying so much he had to stop. He gave the animal a drink, then lay down to sleep beneath a bush, using his bag as pillow. Once more he noticed a cold sweat beading his brow. When he awoke, his teeth chattering, it was almost daylight and the horse lay in the middle of the road. He drew closer, ran his hand along its flank to confirm it was dead. He hugged its neck and kissed it. He felt a profound sense of guilt for that death. He also felt that during the course of the night, exposed to the elements and at the mercy of his fever, he'd lost all sense of security from the previous day. He remembered setting off from the castle buoyed with confidence, as though dressed in armour and clutching a spear. Now dawn discovered him, unclothed and unarmed, fearful of things he had not even remotely considered on his departure. In the first place, he was afraid of dealing with people. The servants, according to Alma, had spread slanderous accusations in the village. He feared the episode that had occurred on his doorstep after the funeral would repeat itself, perhaps even on a greater scale. And what if by this stage he had the whole village against him?

He waited until sunset before walking to the notary's house, with his face half-covered. There the nephew and secretary greeted him, smoking a pipe which exuded the most exquisite aroma. How long was it since Broyz last smoked? No matter, he didn't dare ask to participate.

"Senhor Broyz," he heard through the smoke that filled the room, "we've asked you here as a mere formality. As you're well aware, the castle and the Antunes Coelho family belongings are passed to you following your wife's death."

"That's right," Broyz acknowledged, his head lowered, his tone the same as if confessing to a grave sin.

"Nevertheless …" stated the other, and he took a long pause, an overly theatrical gesture considering his duties, "I've received this letter," he continued, showing it to Broyz, who recognized the handwriting at once, "sent by a someone who calls himself Tomás Antunes Coelho, and who claims the will is invalid."

"Oh, that impostor. Yes, I too have received letters from him. But you're not going to tell me …"

"Of course not," interrupted the notary's nephew. "I too am doubtful of the relationship. However, my duties are to serve justice, which obliges me to postpone the definitive surrendering of property until such time as we can together reject these claims. Do you understand?" he asked, giving Broyz a meaningful look.

"I think so," he stammered. He felt a headache coming on, and didn't know whether to attribute it to the bad news, the exertion of the journey or the tobacco smoke.

"Well," said the notary's nephew, holding out the pipe, which Broyz rejected after a moment's hesitation. If the offer had been made a minute before, before his head started to ache, he would have accepted. "As you can imagine, Senhor Broyz, in view of this last minute complication … in view of this previously unaccounted for matter … in short, you must understand this obliges me to take further measures and procedures, all of which will affect my fees."

Nothing could be more predictable, thought Broyz, wondering where he would obtain that money. The nephew, as though able to read his thoughts, continued:

"No, Senhor Broyz, don't worry about that for the time being. You'll soon be the wealthiest person in the village, able to pay me."

Something about the nephew's benevolent tone of voice inspired mistrust. Broyz didn't forget, deep down, that in the months prior to the wedding, this very person gratefully accepted his bribe.

"For now," said the nephew, "I suggest you be patient and I advise that under no circumstances should it occur to you to sell any object from the castle until all the procedures are concluded."

"Of course not," confirmed Broyz, glancing out the corner of his eye at his bag. "And tell me, will it take long to conclude these formalities?"

"Oh, no … not long … ten, eleven months. You're in no rush, are you?"

"Ten months!" exclaimed Broyz. He expected the notary's nephew would say two months at the most. This heightened his uncertainty.

"And are you sure it will turn out in my favour?" he decided to ask, after a hesitation.

"Hmm … I'm not sure, but let's say I've every confidence."

They shook hands. Broyz took to the street and moments later, his face half-covered, he arrived at Mister Roger's house. He knocked at the door. A light appeared inside the house, as if the banging had awoken the old Englishman.

"Who is it?" asked an unfamiliar voice from the other side of the door. It wasn't the voice of the old man, nor did it sound like the doctor.

Broyz replied in a whisper, for nearby in the street two villagers were keeping an eye on him, as though, beneath his flimsy disguise, they were suspicious of his identity.

"I can't hear," complained the voice.

Broyz repeated his name in vain; the whispers went unheard.

"Look, it's very late to play such mysteries. If you don't tell me your name, I won't open the door."

"On the contrary: if you don't open the door, I won't tell you who I am," replied Broyz, a little louder.

"Fine, I don't want to know your name. Keep it to yourself," exclaimed the voice. Brusque footsteps could be heard going to the back of the house, and the glimmer of light at the window disappeared.

The two villagers, still there, turned and stared at the covered face, making comments under their breath. Broyz supposed they recognized him, and again knocked at the door, out of fear and with impatience this time.

The small light in the window returned and the voice said:
"Okay, that's enough now."

"Please, open, please," Broyz entreated.

"I can't open my door to anyone."

"I'm not anyone. It's me, it's me …" said Broyz, biting his lips
to prevent himself from saying his name.

When the door finally opened and Broyz uncovered his face,
the two men contemplated one another, trying to remember
where they had seen each other before.

"You … you're Broyz, from the castle," the man said at last,
making sweeping gestures. Broyz was so afraid of being recognized, the very sound of his name spoken by another was
enough to make him shudder. However, he didn't like to feel
at a disadvantage. That person knew his name, whereas he
barely remembered the face.

"I'm Broyz, that's correct, and you are?"

It was risky to admit his identity, but he could think of no
other way of ascertaining the name.

"My name's Luís Agua. You may recall Mister Roger
introduced us some time ago, at the auction."

"Yes, I recall that. And where's Mister Roger?" Broyz asked.

"He must be in London by now."

"He's gone? And so you've bought his house."

"Not exactly. Let's just say Mister Roger has left me in
charge," Agua answered. It was simple: as the Englishman had
not managed to sell the house because of his hurried departure,
he told Luís Agua to move in, and join Dr Alves, who still
occupied the guest-room. The problem with Alves was that he
travelled a great deal. At that moment, for example, he was
away for two weeks in Caminhos. The Englishman was afraid
the house would remain empty, especially in view of what had
taken place with the trespassers at Broyz's house.

"So you're in charge …" repeated Broyz. He took a quick
glance inside and concluded that everything was identical to
when the Englishman lived there: the same paintings, the same
dark furnishings. It was, without doubt, the most beautiful
house in Vila Natal. In the middle of the living room, for

example, there stood a rectangular table upon which the Englishman—or perhaps Agua?—had placed two small white busts back to back, their stone eyes looking out in opposite directions, towards the mirror, slightly mottled through damp, that covered a whole wall and gave the illusion of another room, or towards the corridor leading to the bedroom.

Some bottles containing small ships, that lay to one side of the white busts, grabbed Broyz's attention. Many were empty, but others contained a ship. Broyz was surprised the vessels were much bigger than the necks of the bottles. How were they introduced?

"I insert them folded, and then unfold them once they are already inside by pulling on some threads," Agua explained, although the multitude of his gestures only succeeded in distracting Broyz's attention.

How was it possible that a man with such flamboyant gestures, a man larger than life, could withdraw into a pursuit that demanded such concentration, thought Broyz? Watching his vigorous movements, it seemed impossible. Just as the ships seemed inappropriate inside those bottles, Agua too seemed out of place in that house lived in by Mister Roger for so many years.

"I assume, therefore, it's you to whom I should sell these objects," said Broyz, pointing at his bag. Firstly, he established his one condition: nobody here, nor in Coimbra or Lisbon, must know that these objects belonged to the castle.

"Senhor Broyz, I'm more than aware of the warnings. Mister Roger gave me precise instructions before leaving."

"Perfect. Would you be so kind as to say how much you'd give me for this?" and he emptied the contents of the bag onto the same table on which lay the bottles and ships.

Agua ignored the objects and, changing the subject abruptly, offered him something to eat. As Broyz had gone the night and day without so much as a mouthful, he accepted readily. No sooner had he eaten than the fever took hold anew. Agua realized as much for he let slip a comment about his skin, which was so pallid it appeared to be, as he said, "covered in dust." In times of plague everyone conceals their discomfort, and Broyz did just that, arguing he only felt exhausted because of the journey.

"Stay here the night, in the living-room armchair," Agua suggested, "and tomorrow we'll talk calmly."

The following morning, the little ships were no longer on the table, and neither was the bag nor the contents from the castle. Only the busts remained and, in place of the rest, a large bowl of coffee.

While Broyz sipped his coffee, Agua walked around the room, his sweeping gestures dominating the scene.

"I don't know how much you expect for all this, but ever since the epidemic has taken hold, the sale of works of art has decreased. People are no longer amused by luxuries. Forgive me for being so frank, Broyz, but you're crazy if you hope to survive the epidemic by selling ornaments, figurines and knifes and forks. It's as if I wanted to become rich by selling miniature ships. I've another proposal for you. Promise me you'll give me your full attention."

Agua talked with a great deal of aplomb, as though he'd reflected for weeks upon what he was about to say. He spoke of founding a sort of autonomous state behind the low wall surrounding the castle that would safeguard the health of the notables. He mentioned *The Republic* and other old books Broyz had not heard of. What deeply irritated Agua was that Friar Teresino had discriminated against several sick people a few days ago, accepting into the parish ("the house of God," Agua declared, dismayed) only those whom he considered the "most needy." It was understandable that he gave preference to the poor peasants, but it was serious that he insultingly rejected all those "capable of paying for medical treatment from their own pockets," in the friar's words. Such was the case of the veterinary surgeon, Pedro Soares Vilar, and his wife, Ana, who had asked for shelter in the parish, not for economic or medical motives, but rather "for profoundly spiritual reasons," said Agua. And so, given Friar Teresino's uncompassionate attitude, the Soares Vilars were organizing a form of refuge in a large house in Vila

Natal for the sick turned away by the church. One thing was sure: even if the friar were to modify his discriminatory attitude, the huts would soon be unable to house all the infected.

"Friar Teresino," he said, after a pause, "is mixing politics with charity. It's plain to see he only gives refuge to those in his group."

"His group?"

Broyz was not up to date with the disputes between "illuminatists" and "obscurantists," and quickly lost patience with Agua's accusations.

"So, in short, what's your proposal?"

"When I heard about the house for the sick founded by Soares Vilar, I imagined a refuge for all those still in good health. One idea gave way to another, you see. So, I spoke to Doctor Xavier. He agreed and we both shared the view that your castle is the perfect place, far from the centre of infection."

"And what makes you think I'll accept this madness?"

"There are a number of reasons, my friend. For example, you need the money and we, the guests, would pay you for the use of the castle. I've already told you only the wealthy would be involved, so you can expect a mountain of banknotes. Stimulating, isn't it? Another reason is that, currently, you have a dreadful reputation. Well, none of the guests would ever reveal anything about the payment; on the contrary, we would be prepared to say you unselfishly offered to lodge us, and in that way we'd improve your enfeebled reputation."

"I can't believe it," murmured Broyz. "Are these your best reasons?"

"In truth, there are others. We could, for example, install electricity at the castle. What do you think? We still have time to make plans. For the moment, I must advise that until you accept, I can't buy these objects you've brought. I'm sorry, dear Broyz, but we're totally committed to staying there. Assure me, at least, you'll think about my proposition."

"I don't have much to think about. I'll find another buyer," said Broyz. He collected the bag Agua had lain aside on the drawers and left for the castle.

That same afternoon, Doctor Alves returned from Caminhos and learnt of Broyz's visit to the village from Agua. "And so he's recovered?" he thought, and decided to venture to the castle to satisfy his curiosity.

Barely into the journey, indeed after only a few minutes, Alves saw a body lying by the roadside. "Pull up," he yelled at the coachman. Jumping down, he ran towards the man lying face down. His astonishment increased when he turned him over: the man was Broyz. With utmost care, he gathered him up, and though he was heavy, as if he'd swallowed stones, Alves managed to load him into the carriage. Back at the castle, Alma, Alves and the coachman tried to carry Broyz to his bed in the battlement tower. The spiral staircase was so narrow, however, they only managed to reach the first landing before Broyz became stuck, unable to go up or down. Eventually, Alves decided to manage him alone and staggered to the bedroom on the second floor, where Fernanda had previously been cared for.

They sent the coachman on his way, and hurried back to Broyz, who was still alive. While they tried their best to reduce his fever, Alma confessed to the doctor that a few days before she had made up a story about his bedside visit and as a result Broyz had ventured to the village. Alves laughed, promised to be discreet, and asked her a favour in exchange that concerned the plan made by Agua and the other notables.

The doctor asked: help us to convince Broyz—understand it's the only solution for you both—don't tell him I spoke to you of the plan—he is ill, but we'll still let him live among healthy people—if you accept, I'll stay and Broyz will have all the care he needs.

In his eagerness to convince Alma, Alves also spoke of his suspicions concerning Fernanda's death: the symptoms were confusing, it could be African fever, it could be cholera, or some unknown illness.

"African fever?" Alma repeated, surprised.

When Broyz came round, he found the doctor standing at the head of his bed. "How am I? What has happened?" he wanted to know, but Alves placed a finger on his lips, advising him to remain quiet.

The next day, the doctor appeared with a pen and notebook, its pages full of diagrams and observations.

"Can I ask you some questions?"

Broyz inferred that Alves was keeping a kind of statistical record of the village's state of health, but he was wrong. The questions had nothing to do with health matters, but with the climate and the state of the sky. According to a theory he'd evolved, the strength of the epidemic was linked to the absence of clouds.

"It hasn't rained since last year ... there have been no clouds since the middle of May. Did you realize? You didn't realize, true? Nobody realizes, but we've had a clear sky for almost ninety days, and, believe me, these illnesses will not end until it rains or the sun becomes clouded."

Broyz stared at him in surprise. In spite of his obsession for looking out with the binoculars, he hadn't paid any attention to that phenomenon.

"Perhaps it happened before, at another time, two or three months passing without clouds," Alves continued. "Perhaps it happened without anyone noticing. Anyway, I need to know if there were clouds during the days I was away. For example," he took a quick glance at the notebook, "on Wednesday the 9th, Thursday the 10th, Thursday the 24th, and Friday the 25th ... perhaps either of you may remember?"

"There were no clouds, of course there were no clouds," said Alma.

The doctor closed his notebook, satisfied his observations had been confirmed. He accepted a cup of tea that Alma prepared, issued fresh instructions for Broyz to rest and then left the castle for the village.

"It is quite obvious, my children, what God longs for: clear weather and no other light than from the sky above," said Friar Teresino in his Sunday sermon. "Have you realized? We've been weeks without a cloud in the sky. We, ourselves, are the creators of this climate! It's our faith that has chased away the clouds. And this naked sky is the shield with which God has decided to protect us from night and artificial lights." He stood back in the pulpit for a moment, hands crossed behind his back, before returning to his place. "Those promoters of atheism, those pontiffs of an abominable future, tempt us with their abstractions of nature. Nevertheless, is not the absoluteness of the sky an unequivocal message of life? Is it not a divine invitation to work from sundown to sunrise, with all our convictions, and with our complete repudiation of all other lights?"

In spite of the doctor's orders, Broyz rose from his bed as soon as Alma's attention was diverted and mounted the battlement tower in search of his binoculars. It was most unusual, for looking through them from the tower, he would discover objects and landscapes he never saw from the bedroom, as though both rooms belonged to two separate castles.

From the tower, for example, he could clearly see the letterbox. Every morning, Alma would go there to check for a new letter. Broyz followed her footsteps. She walked from the letterbox to the entrance gate, moving discreetly. Was she leaving without warning? Broyz's breath quickened. The binoculars magnified Alma's image with such precision Broyz even imagined he heard the crunch of each footstep. Then it became difficult to see her, trees blocked his view. But after a while, there she was again: stationary, making signals to someone he was unable to see.

"It's them, it's them ..." muttered Broyz, as soon as he thought he recognized some faces. A few days previously, through the binoculars, he managed to see a group of heads behind the trees on the other side of the road. He thought for one moment they were the servants, stalking. Then he realized he'd never seen those faces before. Or was it his fever? He rubbed his eyes and looked once more through the binoculars. They were gone. He rubbed his eyes again, looked: they were there.

"I saw you with them!" he shouted furiously when Alma

returned. "Now I understand. They write the letters and rely on your help. I wouldn't be surprised if a new envelope hadn't been deposited in the letterbox today."

Alma immediately scrunched an envelope she held in her hand, without him realizing. A letter had arrived, but it was pure chance. Those men had nothing to do with her.

"Okay," she said suddenly, " I confess to everything, I'm responsible for those letters ... I deserve to be punished."

She spoke with a sense of irony so unusual for her that Broyz didn't know whether to believe her or not.

"I'm guilty, guilty," she continued, and taking him by the arm, she led him downstairs to the hall. There, she took a seat and, bending over a sheet of blank paper, began to write: "*Dear Senhor Broyz, my name is Tomás Antunes Coelho, I am a relation of the owner of the castle, etc, etc ...*" She imitated Tomás's style. She wrote two or three lines, broke off, and, in a new paragraph, adopted a different handwriting.

"Is this the writing? Or is this one better?" and she continued writing eagerly.

Broyz couldn't bear the situation and disappeared into the tower. He awoke a few hours later with the sun and realized he'd slept in his clothes. He went back down to wash his face, being careful not to make any sound, and discovered a heap of papers on the table in the hall.

He read the first sheets: "*Dear Senhor Broyz, my name ...*" Every three lines the handwriting changed, only the text remained the same. On the reverse of the last page there was another text, this time a letter from Alma.

Vila Natal, 2 April 1923

Dear Broyz,
When morning comes, I will have left for Coimbra. I leave here, along with these papers, the last letter from this Tomás, in which for the first time he notes an address in Coimbra in the hope of a reply. While I was trying uselessly to copy his writing I decided to track down this Tomás, to discover who he is, to prove that I've nothing to do with his demands nor his letters.

A few lines further down, in another handwriting style, perhaps more in keeping with a friendly tone, just as the previous style had been ideal for a proud one, Alma explained the reasons for her anger, reproaching Broyz with sadness for having hidden from her the possible causes of Fernanda's death (*"perhaps you assumed I would leave if you told me all about the epidemic?"*). Lastly, in yet another handwriting, more appropriate for giving advice, she suggested Broyz accept Agua's proposal.

Broyz, as was logical, accepted. There was little by way of alternative. But, most surprising of all, at the end of her letter, in one final change of handwriting, Alma promised to return.

CHAPTER SEVEN

EARLY ONE MORNING in May 1923, Doctor Alves set out for
the castle to inform Broyz the village notables would arrive
that same afternoon. The contract agreed between Broyz and
Alves, signed by both parties in a document setting out the
tenancy rights, stipulated that "Senhor Pedro Broyz welcomes
to the castle, Senhores Luís Agua, Xavier Alves and Paulo
Amaral, along with Senhora Rosa Elsa Amaral, all of whom
will be lodged until the end of the epidemic, following which
they will return to their homes without claims of any kind on
the castle and possessions therein." No reference was made to
any sum of money, so that no-one should have proof of any
payments and everyone would therefore believe in Broyz's
goodwill, the contract indicating that "during the period of the
epidemic, medical decisions will be taken exclusively by Doctor
Alves, decisions directly pertaining to the castle by Senhor
Pedro Broyz, and the remaining questions of community to be
settled between all the guests."

As the sun was setting, two carriages arrived at the castle: one
bearing Agua and the Amarals; the other, outfits, clothes,
blankets and bed linen, as well as provisions, just as Broyz had
requested. A sick horse drew each of these carriages. They
were the last horses in the village and would die shortly as a
result of their efforts.

As agreed, the new arrivals were assigned to rooms furthest
away, in other words, rooms that for centuries had corre-
sponded to servants quarters. To Broyz's surprise, the notables
were not in the slightest bit offended to be lodged there, perhaps
because many of their ancestors had served successive masters
of the castle. On the other hand, what they did take offence at
was the chaos in the main hall, the dirt in the corners, and the
neglect of the plants in the park. The overgrown lawn, the
badly pruned, almost dishevelled bushes did nothing but confirm rumours rife in the village about the poor upkeep of the
castle.

For the first few days, living as a community was awkward, for Broyz confined himself to the courteous formalities of "good afternoon," "excuse me," "sleep well," and more or less ignored his guests, exhibiting the same sense of disdain as the servants had subjected him to months before. Soon, however, Broyz's attitude began to modify, especially as the new arrivals constantly expressed their gratitude for his hospitality and offered him several tasty dishes brought from Vila Natal.

To please Broyz, the guests swept and gathered the leaves, tidied the mess in the rooms and changed the dirty sheets. Their confinement, for which they had no choice, presented few diversions other than meals or conversations, reading or household tasks. As a consequence, when the doctor noticed this routine was making the notables apathetic and idle, he rationed food and fixed a strict time-table of activities, designating each guest a series of specific tasks, many quite absurd in reality, but nevertheless effective remedies against paralysis.

As opposed to the others, the only person authorized to leave the confinement was Alves himself, who every now and again would walk to the village to look after the infected. Statistics occupied the rest of his time: numbers ill, classed by sex, age, states of convalescence, and, of course, calculations and further calculations about the clouds. The pages in his notebook recorded the cloudless sky.

20th May: Vila Natal cloudless.
21st May: Vila Natal cloudless.
22nd May: Vila Natal cloudless.
23rd May: Vila Natal cloudless.
24th May: Vila Natal cloudless.
25th May: Vila Natal cloudless.
26th May: Vila Natal cloudless.
27th May: Vila Natal cloudless,

and so on.

The doctor observed, to his surprise, that despite the absence of clouds the ground remained mysteriously damp. And then he discovered that every two or three nights the sky darkened quickly, allowing a fleeting and silent rainfall. From that moment on, he started to note:

"Vila Natal cloudless by day."

Early one Sunday, however, the others in the castle awoke to his cries. "A cloud," he exclaimed, overwhelmed with joy. It was only one, a very small one. It resembled a feather. Everybody thought others would appear, but nothing followed. The cloud seemed so emaciated, almost translucid, that it became the subject of discussion. Was it indeed a cloud or nothing more than a trace of smoke? If it was, in fact, a cloud, that meant they had to reconsider. The cloud, or whatever it was, didn't manage to cover the sun. In fact, it appeared almost on the sly, so far away on the edge of the horizon that only somebody many kilometres to the west would lose sight of the sun as a result. In consequence, Alves did not acknowledge this cloud, or whatever it was, and continued to count the days of open sky as though nothing had happened. Nevertheless, Agua considered this short-lived apparition to be a good omen. And so it was, for the following day another object appeared in the sky, this time the little aeroplane belonging to Acevedo.

Something was wrong with the aeroplane. The death rattles of its engine could be heard: zac zap mmm mmm. From its tail spewed sparks and sporadic puffs of smoke. The captain landed as best he could, and in so doing visibly damaged the under-carriage and a propeller. The engine had failed and the machine seemed destroyed. Acevedo would have to repair it with what few tools existed in the castle.

As soon as he extricated himself from the plane, Broyz and Agua informed him about the latest events. "We must hide the machine in the stable," said Alves. "It's forbidden to enter or leave the zone, and that includes by air." The captain, who had arrived from Spain, knew nothing about the epidemic and the blockade, still less of Fernanda's death and the changes at the castle. The news upset him more than Broyz would have imagined.

"May I at least stay here peacefully, without risk of infection?" he asked, somewhat confused. Against the wishes of Broyz, who didn't want any more guests, they assigned him one of the bedrooms.

The aeroplane soon aroused more admiration than the electricity had done. The invention of lights offered little or nothing when compared to the invention of the aeroplane, an invention that was capable of making a mockery of the road-blocks and carrying everybody beyond the "plague frontier." By this point, even Broyz seemed to have forgotten Agua's promises to electrify the castle.

To counteract such expectations levelled at his machine, now the sudden saviour, the captain adopted the custom of evening storytelling, while at the same time seeking to revive the motor. He hoped to gain time. Thus, after dinner, as they sat around the table pestering him with questions about the necessary adjustments, Acevedo made recourse to the strategy of exhuming old anecdotes. And though at the beginning he touched on banal subjects that barely caught the attention of the guests, one evening when he happened to mention he knew all the details of the castle's history, he succeeded in kindling everybody's curiosity. "Tell us," said Luís Agua, and the others joined in the request. The old friendship between the aviator and Antunes stimulated their imaginations.

To begin with, the captain told the history of the Antunes Coelho family. It was tedious in parts, though an especially interesting incident occupied the first two nights. Acevedo jumped from branch to branch of the family tree which, according to what he said, had adopted the custom of uniquely employing four names for the men in the family, namely, Jayme, Paulo, João and Pedro, for century after century, generation after generation. "Great-grandfather Paulo informed his brother João that Paulo, Pedro and Jayme, sons of Pedro, were not to quarrel over the lands with their cousin Paulo," Acevedo attempted to explain, even though it was inevitable the listeners would muddle up the relationships.

With the passing of the years, the Antunes family started to thin, partly as a result of the wars, and partly as a result of previous epidemics, and so the family members decided to combine the four names into pairs: João Pedro, Paulo Jayme, Paulo Pedro, etc, etc.

The late Antunes, the person responsible for the will, already bore three of these names, when, foreseeing the imminent decline of his line, he sought permission to add the fourth, "as a conscious way of enclosing the tradition," maintained the aviator.

Parting with tradition, Friar Teresino himself had authorized the addition of a name and had celebrated, unbeknown to the village, the second baptism of the parishioner, Antunes Coelho.

"How do you know all this?" asked Senhora Amaral.

"How do I know?" repeated Acevedo. "You have to remember our families, I mean the Antunes and the Acevedos families, have always been united through warrior spirit. My grandfather Francisco was a soldier, and so was my great-grandfather Mauro. Since bygone days there was always an Acevedo in the front line of this castle's army. Of course, times have changed. There are no longer such men, and armies obey different codes. We live in a modern age, a scientific age. Forgive me if I still believe in the warrior spirit."

"And what do you understand by warrior spirit?" Alves asked, hoping the aviator would loosen up more.

"A warrior is one thing. A soldier is something altogether different. The soldier is a degraded warrior, corrupted by the spirit of industrialization. He's an abstract warrior, appeased by the science of gunpowder. The soldier was created by the State for combat against castles," pronounced the aviator as though quoting someone else's text from memory. Afterwards, he laughed out loud and changed the subject.

Late at night when everybody had gone to sleep, Acevedo went back to repairing his aeroplane in the stable. He often started up the engine, as the mechanics advised, to prevent deterioration from disuse, and with an ominous clatter, the park, foundations and walls of the castle would seem to shake. When Broyz noticed some cracks in the walls and the spiral staircase that led to the tower, he attributed the damage immediately to the vibrations of the plane, but this accusation appeared as nonsense to the captain. He remembered those cracks from decades before and began to expound an unusual theory about damage caused by engine vibrations. With a gesture of impatience, Broyz interrupted and ordered him to stop turning on "his bloody engine" at nights, before going off into the park, grumbling away.

If Acevedo let the matter go, it was only because for a number of days Broyz seemed more irritable than usual, more jealous about the castle's riches that lay for all to see. In short, Broyz wondered how long Alves would take to control the epidemic so that they would leave him alone once and for all. Yet the doctor was unable to give him much assurance, no matter how he boasted of a certain potion made of laudanum that he'd concocted as a remedy against the disease and which he supplied to everyone at the castle. To make matters worse, the potion had such a repugnant taste, Agua alone dared to drink the whole dose while the others chucked it down the drains or out the windows as soon as the doctor's back was turned.

As for the aeroplane, repairs progressed slowly, particularly in comparison to the vertiginous speed of the evening stories.

The following afternoon, after the fifth night of tales, and advancing well into history, Acevedo completed the initial adjustments and set off on a short flight to test the propeller. Of course there wasn't much petrol and it couldn't be wasted, but neither could he venture forth blindly without first testing his machine. And so, climbing into the sky, he discovered the motor was still blocked, zac zap zac, stuttering and spewing a column of jet-black smoke so thick he could, if he wished, trace letters and shapes.

He first drew a rectangle, then completed a triangle and, to finish, he attempted an irregular shape. Then he had the idea to cloud the sun with the smoke ejected by the aeroplane, but the motor started to fade. Mmm zac mmm. Once again, sparks. The propeller jammed. Even so, a pilot of his expertise could land without further mishaps, reduced to gliding, applying his knowledge about thermal currents. Everyone applauded joyfully when he eventually touched down. Doctor Alves promised to note the artificial clouds in his notebook.

"I'm going to develop a method of creating smoke clouds that cover the whole sky. Then the sun will give some respite and the epidemic will abate," Acevedo announced that same night, before returning to the stable to study the motor and the cause of the smoke. Three nights passed without his stories. During the day, he traced clouds with strange silhouettes. It didn't take much to outline the contours, though just as quickly the wind would disperse them, and he would return to the sky to take care of every cloud that threatened to disappear, each with a different sketch: one for the cirrus, another for the stratos, and yet another for the cumulus.

Of course, in no time, this winged Sisyphus bored everyone with his celestial tracings that never enough to cloud the sun. On the fourth night Alves and Agua presented themselves at the stable, interrupting his machinations.

"Your warrior spirit seems to have succumbed to the enchantment of science, Acevedo dear friend. Instead of re-pairing the aeroplane or putting into practice an escape plan, you're inventing cloud machines."

Acevedo frowned and delayed his reply. He walked towards his aeroplane, extracted from the cockpit a large sheet of paper rolled like an old parchment and slowly unfolded his plan for a water mirror.

"All the rain that falls at night will be evaporated by daytime, forming condensation clouds. The sun will go away and it'll mean an end to the epidemic. You'll thank me later."

"Please, Captain. The plane is the only means of escape," replied Agua.

"Escape?" Acevedo laughed and shook his head.

"Do as you wish. Construct one, two, a hundred water mirrors, but first repair the aeroplane," urged Alves, who had spent the past week installing huge awnings in the park as protection from the sun.

Acevedo grunted something or other under his breath and returned the plan to the cockpit.

For three days he looked for an ally for the enterprise of constructing, with pick and shovel, a large pond in the middle of the park. Not far away from the castle, everyone told him, there was a stream that did nothing to create clouds. As Acevedo refused to acknowledge this, he continued blindly with his project. Meanwhile, the others withdrew into equally useless and solitary tasks: walking in silence, sleeping under the awnings beneath the burning sun, reading old books with yellowish pages. They exchanged no more words than necessary, as though conserving their energies for the resumption of the nightly gatherings.

Sometimes Alves would leave the castle and walk to the village to tend the very ill, easing their pain. Although nobody asked how things went, it was enough to see his face on his return to understand the epidemic still gained ground.

On one occasion Broyz accompanied Alves to the village. His pulse was trembling, partly because the disease had already weakened him, and partly because setting foot in the village once more re-awakened his fear of being lynched. The doctor found Broyz's efforts of such little use he never again asked for his company.

After that journey, Alves noticed Broyz's fever had worsened. As he had kept hidden from everyone that their host had been infected since before the contract was drawn up, he was especially concerned that Agua or the Amarals might discover his deception. What would they say when they found out? Would they understand that Broyz's infection had been the price to pay for refuge in the castle?

Soon Broyz no longer behaved like someone whose fever rose on occasions, but like someone whose fever never diminished. He didn't open the large windows. He didn't come down from the tower other than for meals or story-nights. He was the master of the castle, but he lived in the tower in self-imposed isolation. Nothing, not even the memory of Alma, managed to stir him. He'd received three letters in the first few days, just prior to the arrival of Acevedo: two letters from this Tomás; the other from Alma. "I promise I'll find out who Tomás is. Then I'll return." Perhaps Alma had written him other letters from Coimbra, but if nobody in Vila Natal was able to stay on their feet, how could he expect a messenger to reach the castle.

As for Agua and the Amarals, they seemed delighted to do nothing. Unlike Broyz, they didn't hide away in the shade, but preferred to walk off their profound boredom in the park, even avoiding looking at one another.

One night, Luís Agua asked the doctor if he would take advantage of his next excursion into the village to make a quick stop at the house in Rua Simões.

"There's a suitcase hidden under the floor of the kitchen. Just lift some loose floorboards," he explained with his usual disproportionate gestures.

Alves went to the village on three occasions and each time returned without the suitcase.

"The house appears to be lived in. Nobody answers my calls and the door is locked," he informed Agua after his third visit.

Nonetheless, two or three days later Alves appeared with the suitcase.

"What is this?" asked Agua on seeing its contents. "I don't understand … Where's the lighting generator?"

The suitcase contained three bottled ships, eight empty bottles and other implements to make miniatures. Had Alves risked confronting the trespassers just for this?

Not for that alone. Apart from the suitcase, whose original contents someone had obviously confiscated and replaced with those trifles, the occupants had handed Alves a letter from the Electricity Company. Bad news: Luís Agua was "sanctioned for professional negligence," such was the opinion of Senhor Rubem Pereira, the Portuguese representative for the firm of Douglas & Banks. It didn't specify what type of sanction had been dealt, but it urged him, on the other hand, to present himself "urgently" at the Lisbon central office, since Senhor Pereira considered his "silence and disappearance" to be a severe act of rebellion.

Obviously, Senhor Pereira knew nothing about the "plague

frontier." It was also quite apparent to Broyz that despite the epidemic, the postal service was still in operation, and if, until then, he'd found justification for Alma's lack of correspondence, he now wondered why she wasn't writing any more letters from Coimbra, not even a few lines.

Next day, Agua returned to his hobby of miniature models, only now, instead of ships, he began to make a small replica of Acevedo's aeroplane.

"How will you manage to fit the aeroplane into the bottle?" asked Alves, seeing him put the final touches to the wings. It was always the same: each time someone learnt about his miniatures, he would have to explain the secret.

"Come … look … I'll give you a demonstration," said Agua.

And then, as he prepared to fold the wings and slide the model into the glass bottle, the stable shook with the roarings of the big aeroplane, the real one.

They all ran in the direction of the noise, where Acevedo, his plan for the water-mirrors thwarted, once more sported his overalls and goggles.

"And if I fix the aeroplane, who'll travel with me? Don't forget, gentlemen, there's only space for two on board."

Agua and Alves looked at each other for a response. Both understood the airman had regained control of the situation.

That same night while Agua, Broyz and Alves tried to reach an agreement, the captain related the story of the marriage between Antunes and Fernanda.

Antunes Coelho, according to Acevedo, had been forced to marry through parental pressure. He was an only son and, as the elder generation of the dynasty was dying away, so the unthinkable loss of the family name seemed likelihood.

One day the Antunes family decided, without consulting their son, that Fernanda Magalhães Sequeira, a pretty young girl from Lisbon, and the daughter of a prosperous shipping company owner, was the ideal wife to bear João Paulo's children and thus continue the line. They travelled to the capital, finalized the details with her parents, and returned to the castle with the young girl and her governess. In view of the gaping age difference between the husband, who was over thirty years old, and the girl, who was in truth only a young child of fifteen, the families agreed that Fernanda would live in the Castle, without marrying, until her seventeenth birthday. The situation of the Magalhães, continued the captain, was not so different to that of the Antunes family. They were elderly, Fernanda was their only daughter, and they wanted little else for her than a convenient marriage.

Fernanda arrived at Vila Natal on a cold January morning and settled in the room in the battlement tower, usually reserved for guests. In the afternoon, while exploring her immediate surroundings, she saw two young men in the distance. "They're waving," said the governess. "Waving?" asked Fernanda, and to gain a closer look, she raised the binoculars given by her mother. "They certainly are waving ... and they're coming this way," she giggled, not disguising her excitement. Which of the two was her husband-to-be?

Before she had time to compose herself, the two young men were shaking her hand. Although they looked similar, and someone who had not known otherwise would have said they were brothers, one of them was more self-assured and spoke more eloquently.

"You mustn't tell Senhor and Senhora Antunes you've already met," the governess advised. "It was intended you should not see each other until this evening at the presentation dinner." The men replied together: "We won't say a word, don't worry." The governess burst out laughing. "How amusing," she said, "they answer as one, as if they were both going to marry the girl." Yet, the observation, even though intended to be humorous, far from enlivened that first encounter. It seemed to inhibit the two young men, who went off hastily, glancing at one another out of the corner of their eyes.

The girl and the governess continued their walk in silence.

"He's charming, this young man Acevedo," said Fernanda suddenly, implying unintentionally that Antunes was perhaps less so.

By the time Fernanda turned seventeen her parents had died and she had been there long enough to discover that, in fact, Acevedo was not only more to her liking, but also more handsome than her future husband. Yet it was no good bemoaning the situation to her faithful governess. "In my opinion, my dear, you must first fulfil the wishes of your deceased parents. Once you're married, everything will be different. What's more, if I may say, I believe that even though Acevedo is very fond of you too, he's so loyal to his best friend he would never admit it to himself."

"I'm unhappy," insisted Fernanda.

"Please, my dear, you must marry Antunes Coelho. Once you're married you'll see how things take care of themselves." Of course, at that age, Fernanda didn't understand what the woman was insinuating, that she already imagined the young girl in twenty years time as the wife of one, the lover of the other.

The wedding did not produce the results everyone had expected.

Initially, nobody was alarmed when Fernanda failed to become pregnant. "She's so young," Senhor and Senhora Antunes would say. Yet, before long, João Paulo's father died, and his mother fell ill, and nobody despaired more than the husband who, like so many men, accused his wife of being sterile. She, who also longed for a son, retorted energetically with the slight: "Bring me a man, any man, young and strong, and I'll show you I can be a mother." Nothing gave Antunes, already mature in years, more of a complex than Fernanda's youthfulness. And so, having considered various alternatives, he sought out his friend Acevedo one night and proposed he become the father of his son. It was not only his idea, but also his sick mother's.

Though honoured by his friend's trust, Acevedo said he had to think about it.

"If it had been anyone but my best friend proposing such a thing, I would've insulted him that very moment. Clearly, Fernanda was a beautiful woman, I didn't deny that, and the arguments Antunes brandished, such as his desire to preserve the family name, were very valid, but at the same time the whole thing seemed to me immoral, above all because I sensed Fernanda had never been consulted."

The next day Broyz could think of nothing else but the story. True or false, it seemed in fact an immodest act, an indiscretion, that the aviator should divulge to a haphazard audience the supposed attraction that Fernanda had felt towards him. Yet, what if it was true? Or worse still, what if Fernanda and Acevedo really had been lovers? He succumbed to the idea for a moment. Fernanda and the aviator? His Fernanda? He imagined them together and burst out laughing. He wasn't fond of the airman, but even so, he needed to talk further with him in private, without the others knowing, because a story recounted around the table had intrigued him: if all the men in the Antunes Coelho family had only been named Paulo, Jayme, Pedro or João, was it possible that a Tomás might exist? In order to confirm his suspicions surrounding the authenticity of the letters, Broyz needed to abandon his refuge in the tower, overcome his tremendous drowsiness and pluck up courage to talk to Acevedo. It seemed straightforward, but he was incapable of it.

The following night, the tenth of the gatherings, was the most eagerly awaited.

"What happened? Did you make a deal with Antunes Coelho?" asked Alves.

"Of course not," replied Acevedo. "It was unacceptable. However, Antunes and his mother didn't tolerate my refusal. They ejected me from the castle. I had to leave at once, without any farewells. They slandered me in Fernanda's eyes, telling her I was expelled for being a thief. Only many years later, when Antunes' death was a distant memory, could I regain her trust."

"And what became of you, beyond the castle?" asked Amaral.

What was taking place demonstrated Acevedo's talent for captivating and electrifying his audience.

"It's a long story," the captain sighed.

And it turned out he had spent two years in Lisbon, before

settling down in Porto, in the house of a certain Resende, an ex-policeman whom he'd known previously in Vila Natal.

Resende rented him a small room in return for a meagre sum and the condition that Acevedo would look after his house when he was away on business. The months passed and Acevedo did nothing: he had no job, scarcely went out, and rarely spoke with his host. What job could an old warrior like him find in a new era that appeared scientific in the extreme? A colleague of Resende informed him that servants in the small castles in France were well paid and had a preference for men with experience in other castles. This meant serving duties, the very idea of which provoked nausea. Avecedo still had some savings, enough to live for nine or ten years without undue problems. When the money ran out he would be forty-eight. He imagined he would live a long life, since all his ancestors had lived well into their seventies. It was imperative he increased his savings by working for at least three or four seasons.

Resende, on the other hand, didn't have these problems. Since the police force he'd taken up dozens of positions: detective, secretary, personal bodyguard to a high-ranking military man, laboratory helper, and even post-office employee, dealing with the public or dispatching parcels. Of all his jobs, he preferred the one he had then, piloting a post-office aeroplane between France, Spain, Portugal and various cities in North Africa.

The aeroplane belonged to the same military man for whom Resende had worked as secretary. The post-office contracted the services of the aeroplane and its owner had chosen Resende for being efficient and trustworthy.

"When I accepted the job, I did so as though it were the most natural thing in the world," Resende explained to Acevedo. "I was only interested in the pay. I'd never flown before and had to learn in a matter of weeks. A French instructor, visiting the region, trained me. I can still recall the bewilderment of that first flight. I couldn't believe what it was like to see things from the air. My first night flight later was simply unforgettable. So we didn't lose our way, someone from the post-office had given money to six or seven peasant families, spread out from the departure point to the place of arrival. These country folk had to light huge bonfires to guide us. It was very risky. It only needed one bonfire to go out, or one family not to fulfill its agreement, for us to be lost in the night sky. Look at it like this: the peasants were helping, having never seen an aeroplane close up, without really understanding anything. For them, that object known as an aeroplane was nothing more than a dot in the sky. This added to their irresponsibility because they were unaware of the purpose of the bonfires and just how much was at stake if they forgot to light them or if the flames went out. As far as the size of the aeroplanes was concerned, I wonder what they could've imagined. Everything was possible seen from below, more so when they were unaware of the height at which we were flying. It was impossible to judge the altitude without knowing the size of the aeroplane, and vice-versa. I suppose the aeroplanes, or rather, the moving dots they managed to see, could well have looked like enormous machines flying high, or small machines flying low, depending on their uninformed perspective."

"What's strange," reflected Resende, "it's that I'd never planned on becoming a pilot. I'd dreamt of becoming a musician, or perhaps even a famous general … although, of course, when I was fifteen years old, aereoplanes hadn't been invented. How could I therefore have dreamt of a non-existent profession? Now we can fly. We're very privileged, Acevedo, my friend. We're witnessing the most momentous changes in our civiliza-tion. I've no idea what these changes will bring, but you'll see, I think, that time, for some reason, has speeded up. In other words we, you and I, could live two lives … provided we dare. I'm prepared to. I spent the first part of my life in candlelight, on board tumbledown carriages; now I'm living a second life of aeroplanes and electricity, radio and cinema. We'll pass away, leaving behind a world completely alien to the one we were born into. Something like this was inconceivable for our forefathers. Do you follow me?"

Acevedo, in general, followed Resende's reasoning with misgiving, as if the retired policeman hardly knew what he was

109

talking about. However, this particular discussion kindled his enthusiasm because of its defence of adventure. The many years in that massive stone construction hadn't killed his warrior spirit. He was happy to be made aware of it. A few days later, when Resende invited him on a short trip to Lisbon, Acevedo accepted. He climbed into the aeroplane seemingly unfazed, though in truth he was trembling with fear. He climbed down another man, his head swimming with visions. A month later, Resende invited him again. This time it was a far more extensive voyage … to Paris.

In Paris, during the first months of 1914, the war seemed far away and, at the same time, imminent. Parisians talked about the feats of Blériot, Humet and Prier, and the inauguration of the postal air-service between England and France. The whole city was in the grips of "aeroplane fever." In a cabaret in Montmartre, a black dancer treated the public to the "dance of the aviator," spreading her arms like the vibrating wings of an aeroplane as she stepped over a huge map of dazzling colours. When the Captain got wind of the show, he decided to see for himself. There she stood, a large white propeller fastened to her chest, a knot of ribbons, with a dark face beneath a red hat shaped as a monoplane.

On leaving the cabaret, Acevedo ambled through the streets of the centre, along the banks of the Seine, and stopped awhile before the Eiffel Tower. He looked up, casting his eye over that iron monument which, in a remote way, echoed the massive constructions made of stone. He had no doubts. A new era summoned him. All the money at his disposal was not enough to buy even the smallest aeroplane, but Resende offered to pay the substantial difference and form a partnership. They would operate an aeroplane together, as a postal airline, just like Resende's boss. If all went well they would dedicate themselves to passenger flights, or taking photographs so the cartographers could correct the old maps drawn on the ground from simple intuition. All of that meant good money at that time. At least, so Resende reckoned.

They bought the aeroplane in France. Soon enough they

had offers of work that took them far away to places such as the Canary Islands, or Morocco, where they struck up a friendship with an eccentric French aviator, called Prince, who was in charge of the post at the Moroccan airfield.

Everything went perfectly until one day in August 1917 when Acevedo, who was in Lisbon, received a telegram from Prince: "Resende accident. Urgent voyage to Cap Juby." No sooner had he set foot in Morocco than he learnt the truth. His partner had died near the airfield flight testing the latest model a German pilot had lent him. Miraculously, the German's aeroplane had hardly been damaged. The captain shouldered the repair bill, then returned to Lisbon, where he settled all his pending commitments. Having amassed a modest fortune, including a sum left by his partner, he readied himself to, in his own words, "practice a life of adventures," a life of dilettante voyages which would take him to Prague one day, Athens or Istanbul the next.

"I'm a lucky man, there's no doubt. One has to take advantage of progress in a time when there's no place for the spirit of adventure."

"Hear hear. To progress," Agua proposed, raising his glass. "To electricity!"

"To progress and aviation," corrected the captain.

"Now I understand … let's see …" winked Broyz and began to recite a Triumphal Ode, parodying the work of a fashionable poet of the time.

"*Oh wheels, gears, motors!*
My lips are parched by the noises of modernity
Ah, to be able to express myself like a motor,
To be complete like a machine,
And adventurous like an aeroplane!
Electricity, diseased nerves of Matter
Railways, bridges, propellers and factories
Oh, to be the mechanical heat
And turn, rotate and flow!
To be the whole future within the present
And to leap with everything over everything…"

The clinking of glasses for another toast "to progress" interrupted Broyz's sarcastic recital. At this stage he was still the most sober in the group.

"Enough," requested Doctor Alves. "Here we are in the age of machines, and we still don't know how to rid ourselves of the plague. Forgive me if I decline the toast, but I'd gladly exchange all the inventions you're marvelling about so much for an effective remedy."

And having said that, Alves made a silent gesture that could be interpreted as: "Acevedo's story ends here, we've arrived at the present." Nevertheless, on the two subsequent nights, without Acevedo's leadership, Luís Agua told the story Mister Roger had confided in him three years before, upon their return from the auction. He spoke about the widow and the will. Although everybody knew about that event, nobody dared interrupt, least of all suggest he skip some of the facts. Inexorably, the tale lead to the arrival of Broyz and his marriage to Fernanda, and having reached that point, instead of progressing, the tale became more and more complicated, while Broyz remained silent, ashamed of his story. Why did he say nothing? Why did he allow the facts to be distorted? Purely to provoke him, Alves fabricated an untrue account in which Broyz was disgraced, but on the night he planned to recount it, Broyz missed the gathering. Gradually, his absences became more frequent, and every time a crucial part of his story came around, Broyz remained in the tower, or made excuses to leave the table.

As well as Broyz, the Amarals too began to show signs of infection and had to lock themselves away in their bedroom. Preoccupied about the health of her husband, Rosa Elsa called Doctor Alves and asked him, trembling:

"Will Paulo pull through? Is there any hope?"

"Very little," admitted the doctor, having examined him. Poor Amaral was of such fragile constitution that the pestilence had attacked his organism with greater rapidity than others.

A few days later, at midnight, Paulo Amaral died in the arms of his wife. They buried him straight away for fear of contagion, and Alves recommended they should all drink three or four daily doses of his laudanum syrup for one week.

Captain Acevedo's announcment that the aeroplane had been repaired was not mistimed. He did so, as Alves realized, on the same night as Broyz's story drew to an end. This discovery fascinated the doctor, although he refrained from commenting to the others.

"What shall we do now the aeroplane can fly?" asked Broyz.

Acevedo made no reply.

The following morning Alves, Broyz and Agua were woken by noises. Jumping from their beds, they peeped out to see the aeroplane gathering speed, taking with it Acevedo and Senhora Amaral.

The captain had made up his own mind as to whom deserved the first flight. He hadn't made a bad choice, according to Doctor Alves.

"There's no need to get alarmed. Acevedo will return for the others shortly," said Alves, who thought it appropriate to suspend the storytelling that night. The same the following night, and the next ... At last, since Acevedo failed to reappear, a gathering was called to declare an end to the gatherings.

It was nine o'clock in the evening, Alves and Agua were already seated at table, but Broyz was missing. Without him, the meeting couldn't reach a conclusion since two people cannot constitute a gathering, can it? Everything suggested Alves should annul the gathering yet again when Broyz arrived in the hall dressed from head to toe in white. Looking thin and weak in the baggy clothes of the deceased Antunes Coelho, he appeared like a ghost.

Before Broyz could take a seat, Doctor Alves spoke. He believed the captain had deliberately left the castle at a specific time.

"He left to set us free," he said.

"Set us free?" asked Agua, laughing. "Those of us who are free are himself and Senhora Amaral."

"Let me explain. To have continued, we would have had to retell the night that began the storytelling, don't you see?"

"I don't understand, what should I see?"

"Well, what would have happened? Were we perhaps going to tell the whole story from the beginning once again?"

"I don't understand anything," protested Agua. "You insist that Acevedo has freed us. But what has he freed us from?"

"From a paradox," replied Alves.

"What nonsense," said Luís Agua.

"No, no! Imagine. We would've had to tell within our circle the story told within the circle, and so on ad infinitum," insisted Alves. Broyz replied that he thought he understood what he meant, and that once, in the studio of a painter friend, he'd seen an easel with a painting that depicted an easel with a painting that depicted an easel ...

"The painter told me the technique is known as escape into the abyss. Are you suggesting something like that?"

"Undoubtedly," Alves rejoiced. "Although, in this case, the captain preferred escape in an aeroplane."

"Anyway," insisted Agua, "I'll only say Acevedo has saved us on the day he returns to take us out of here."

CHAPTER EIGHT

BARELY had she arrived in Coimbra than Alma made straight for Rua Ruí Fernandes in search of twenty-one, the number this Tomás had indicated in one of his letters. She found the street easily enough, but not the number. The address this so-called Tomás had given did not exist. In Rua Ruí Fernandes there was a house numbered ten and, further along, another numbered thirty-two. In between, before the wall that linked both houses, a man stood on the pavement. He wore a scraggy beard, battered boots and a filthy shirt. His eyes were hostile with heavy bags, and his nails black. His gestures were hostile, his feet turned in, slightly pigeon-toed. In fact, his general demeanour was hostile, hunched like an old man, even though he was probably a lad of little more than twenty-five.

Alma and the young tramp stood looking at each other for a moment. Under his arm he carried a bundle of papers or something similar. He took a paper and held it out, offering it to her with all the courtesy he was capable of mustering. She stepped forward to take it. It seemed to be a pamphlet, badly printed, scarcely legible.

"I'm looking for someone," she said, slipping the paper into a pocket.

The man opened his arms and raised his eyebrows, saying nothing. Then, struck by an idea, he pointed to the bell-tower of the church of Santa Cruz, just visible from where they stood.

"The church?" asked Alma.

The man nodded. It was custom for the churches of each area to hold a complete register of families.

Alma said goodbye to the tramp and went to check in the church whether a Tomás Antunes Coelho did exist and where it was possible to find him. Nobody by that name existed. Furthermore, the registers showed no living person with that name. Was it true, therefore, that the Antunes Coelho dynasty had come to an end? Something told Alma the answer was not quite so straightforward.

It was getting dark. In Coimbra, there were few hotels, all very expensive. On the other hand, there were plenty of boarding-houses for students that were fairly accessible, although it was quite unlikely they would accept her because of a regulation prohibiting single women from lodging. In addition, Alma looked more like a village girl than a city girl.

"I'm on my way to Lisbon," she lied in order to find a room. "Until yesterday, I worked as a chamber-maid at a grand castle. Now the master has died, and I must present myself at the home of his sister. Please, before I continue on my way, I need to spend a week here settling various matters."

"I'm sorry … I don't think it's advisable," they replied in every boarding-house. She was lost unless she changed her strategy. Then it occurred to her that instead of paying for her stay with money, she could pay for it with work. In that way, she wouldn't be breaking the regulations, for she would be an employee instead of a guest.

"Why not," said the landlady of the fifth boarding-house Alma visited, after pondering the idea for a few minutes. "I'll tell you what we'll do: I'm going to take a week's break, no cooking or scrubbing the floors, no cleaning the bathroom or washing the sheets. I'll take you."

They made up a small bed for her in an attic-room until then only used to house tools and odds and ends. Alma was not especially tall, but this bed was too small, she had to tuck her feet in to fit.

The landlady wished her pleasant dreams, reiterating that a hard day's work awaited her, and placed a burning paraffin lamp on a box to one side of the bed. Although many houses in Coimbra had electricity, this wasn't the case in this boarding-house.

Alma had started undressing when she heard a faint noise, nearby and persistent. It seemed like someone was scratching at the door, perhaps a student aware of her arrival was trying to play with her. As there was no way of locking the attic-room door from the inside, she hurriedly pulled back on her overcoat. "They mustn't sense I'm afraid," she told herself, trembling.

"Courage, courage ... but what can I do?" She took hold of the lamp as a replacement for a more convincing weapon and opened the door forcefully, ready to defend herself from whomever was responsible for those noises. Everything was dark in the corridor leading to the room. Nevertheless, the noises continued, closer than before. Alma felt something at her feet. She looked down and saw a rat, then another ... then two more a few steps away. Another woman would have unleashed a mighty shriek, but she wasn't like those city girls who screamed for nothing.

Calmed, she removed her coat once more and slid between the sheets, at the same time patting a pocket in which she kept Fernanda's bracelet. She had pinched it from the castle in order to have something valuable to pawn in case of emergency. As she felt for the bracelet, she also felt something else in her pocket, the pamphlet the tramp in Rua Ruí Fernandes had given her. She wanted to read it and brought it closer to the lamp. Even though it was badly printed and the light was dim, she thought she recognized the word Broyz. Then she fell asleep, waking in the morning convinced the whole pamphlet episode had been nothing but a dream. "I didn't look properly. It can't be true it says Broyz." The name appeared in several paragraphs, however, amidst words that were impossible to read.

That afternoon Alma worked as she had never done before in the castle. At six, all her tasks finished, she was able to set out for Rua Ruí Fernandes. As the boarding-house was in Rua da Sota, behind the building works for the future Astoria Hotel, she had to climb uphill, past the Almedina arch, to try to locate the tramp. It was already getting dark and there was only a policeman in the street. She asked if he'd seen a man looking like a tramp. He told her that man usually turned up on Mondays and Wednesdays, between one and four.

"What day is it today?" she asked, eagerly.

The policeman looked at her as if she was joking.

"What day? Today's Wednesday, tomorrow's Thursday."

She would have to wait until Monday if she wanted to see the tramp again. It seemed risky, precisely because Monday was the deadline Senhora Moraes, the landlady at the boarding-house, had given. But Alma soon realized the deadline was fairly flexible, since the landlady was delighted with her helper as it allowed her to sleep and enjoy herself a little more. And so, Alma took her courage in both hands:

"Senhora Moraes, next Monday I need to finish my duties earlier than usual, let's say by midday …"

"That wasn't the agreement," protested the woman, bad-temperedly. "There's a lot of work to be done."

"Whatever you say, Senhora Moraes," replied Alma, and immediately set about studying the times when the woman left the boarding-house. She noted that after lunch in the kitchen, at twelve-thirty, Senhora Moraes always went out shortly before two, returning around four, or four-thirty at the latest. Alma hatched a plan. She would leave at three, after her, and would return half an hour later. Nobody would notice her absence, neither the students, shut away in their rooms, bent over their books, nor the woman, who, on her return at four, would find Alma working away unpertubed.

When Monday arrived, Alma put her escape into action. In Ria Ruí Fernandes the young tramp was in the same place as last time, in the same position, wearing exactly the same clothes, although his beard was bushier. She told him she'd read the pamphlet and wanted to ask some questions, but she was again greeted with stubborn silence, interrupted by occasional monosyllables.

"Who is that Doctor Broyz?" asked Alma.

"Don't know."

"Where do the pamphlets come from?"

"Don't know. I get them and give them."

"Who gives them to you?"

"Don't know."

She continued asking further questions, each time receiving the same reply: "Don't know."

Alma estimated her thirty minutes were almost up. She tried in vain to extract some further piece of information before saying goodbye and returning downhill to the boarding-house. Senhora Moraes, however, had returned earlier for once and awaited her on the threshold, arms folded and disbelieving, to warn her she would not tolerate any further irresponsibility. "I beg your pardon, senhora," Alma pleaded and, looking downcast, headed up to her makeshift room to discover someone had stolen her belongings. Who had robbed her? It could equally have been the senhora herself just as much as some student. In any case, all she now possessed was what she had in her overcoat pockets: a few coins, two notes, the pamphlet and the bracelet with rubies, which she had hidden out of fear.

As it was a week since her arrival at the boarding-house, Alma supposed Senhora Moraes would make some comment. Yet, on Tuesday, just as on the seven previous days, she was awoken early to begin cleaning.

In every room there were between four and six beds. The students tended to form groups according to their studies. There was one room with four privileged medical students. There was another with future lawyers. It was always the same in the boarding-house, and so the rooms were given names, Medicine, Law, or Architecture, depending on the courses of the occupants.

Having washed the windows, she went downstairs to prepare the food. On seeing her, the medical students invited her to sit at their table. Despite their kindness and friendly manner, Alma declined the invitation, whereupon Arnaldo, the most talkative of the group, stood and indicated the unoccupied seat with a gesture some way between gentlemanly and impatient. Senhora Moraes was not in the boarding-house at that time, why shouldn't Alma take a seat, at least for a little while?

When she did, Arnaldo and the others started to interrogate her, without meaning to amuse themselves at her expense, but more out of genuine interest to know about her and where she came from.

Alma relayed a good part of her life story, though she took care not to mention Broyz, so as not to contradict the tale she had recounted to Senhora Moraes.

"So what's it like to live in a castle?" asked Carlos, a lad with bags under his eyes.

"So what's it like to live in Lisbon," retorted Alma, and the students who practically all hailed from Lisbon broke out laughing for no good reason.

Talk turned to other matters, and the young men were surprised to learn that Alma was well-informed about life in Coimbra, even knowing the name of the former University rector, they remarked, and all this because Broyz had told her various anecdotes about his student years.

Heartened by their good nature, Alma decided to show them the pamphlet and ask if they had heard of a Doctor Broyz.

"Of course. He's a well-known character," said Arnaldo.

"A non-existent character," Carlos corrected.

"Non-existent?" Alma exclaimed.

"As I understand it," Arnaldo intervened, "this Broyz does indeed exist, and the person responsible for these pamphlets is someone who hates him. The rector's office is looking for him at the real Broyz's request. Some even suspect that ..."

"No, that's nonsense," Carlos interrupted. "Broyz doesn't exist. He's the invention of some joker."

While the students continued arguing, Alma considered the appropriateness of asking for a meeting with the rector to inform him about the young tramp giving out pamphlets in Rua Ruí Fernandes. Inexplicably, however, she felt a sense of pity for him. Besides, it was unlikely the rector would receive her in his office. What would she say to him? That she was Broyz's favourite chamber-maid? That she was his mistress? Alma sensed the tramp knew more than he let on. If she made an accusation to the Rector, they might throw him in prison and she wouldn't be able to speak to him again.

The following day Alma decided to take another trip to Rua Ruí Fernandes. This time she found neither the policeman nor the tramp. Perhaps she should wait until one of them arrived? She would be taking a chance. She had left the boarding-house, taking advantage of the fact that Senhora Moraes had gone for a walk. Although it was clear she couldn't linger long in view of her previous escape, having already taken the risk, another ten minutes wouldn't change anything. She stopped, therefore, at the exact spot where the tramp had been positioned, and, at that moment, she saw something she hadn't noticed from her previous visits: the whitewashed wall which extended from the door of number ten to the door of number thirty-two had small inscriptions carved on it, one of them being a twenty-one, painted black. This number twenty-one, she realized, was in the precise spot she had seen the tramp standing.

The discovery startled her. She felt nauseous, and although she placed her hands against the wall, she couldn't prevent herself from fainting, only managing to lessen the impact of her fall.

When she came round, the tramp was at her side. However, she was not in Rua Ruí Fernandes, nor in Senhora Moraes' boarding-house, but in a sort of basement where the tramp lived.

Alma kept calm, despite being alone with him in the basement and lying on his bed. Her fainting, in contrast, alarmed her. Had she become infected by the epidemic? She was also alarmed at the night sky through the small basement window. Would Senhora Moraes throw her out of the boarding-house? Where would she stay without a *centavo* to her name?

Instinctively, she placed her hand on the inside pocket where the bracelet was hidden.

"Go back to sleep," said the tramp.

She wanted to say something, but it was as if the words stuck in her throat.

At last, she managed to utter, with a wisp of a voice:

"Do I have something serious?"

The tramp looked at her with a beaming smile.

"Serious?" he said, and Alma momentarily feared for the lad's sanity. "Congratulations, congratulations!" he exclaimed.

"Congratulations?"

"Perhaps I'm mistaken, but I suspect you're pregnant," Alma heard, and she felt she was about to faint once more.

Alma had a fever because she had cholera. The tramp kept watch over her because of her pregnancy, plying her with medicaments and remedies. Both the medications and the fever plunged Alma into a form of lethargy where she was delirious, confusing reality with terrifying nightmares. Sometimes she would wake in her own sick, sometimes she would utter incoherent sentences in her dreams. Yet it was this very state that kept her alive.

She had spent almost three months in her bed in the basement when the streets of Coimbra started to choke with the arrival of caravans of sick people driven in from various parts of the region. Although isolated cases of pestilence had been registered in the poorer outskirts, the risks of contamination in Coimbra were less than in villages such as Vila Natal, which was ravaged by the epidemic. Aware of this, and alerted to the government closing off roads to isolate the most infected villages, the villagers fled hastily in groups towards Coimbra, walking, or rather, staggering. From afar these caravans looked like the columns of a vanquished army.

The exodus towards the city didn't provide the sick with the solution they imagined. As none of the boarding-houses accepted strangers for fear of infection, hundreds of villagers took over the ancient ruins of Conimbriga, not far from Coimbra, that dated back to Roman times. In contrast, those who remained in the city wandered the streets and spread out to sleep on pavements or in entrances to houses. To avoid such disorder, the Mayor, João Silva de Rocha, created four large dormitories for the people: the first in the Praça 8 de Maio, opposite the church of Santa Cruz; the second in Jardim de Manga, behind the church; the third in the Praça do Comércio, at the foot of the stairway of San Tiago; and the last, the biggest, on the green swathes adjacent to the Avenida Sá da Bandeira, next to the monument of the fallen in the Great War. Between fifty and eighty new arrivals gathered in each place, sharing out clothes, blankets and medicines. Twenty or so policemen remained on guard to protect the travellers, so they said, although in reality it seemed more likely they were isolating them from the healthy sector of the population, the perspective dependent on how each viewed it.

As rapidly as the country villages became depopulated, the streets of Coimbra found themselves packed. Such a situation inevitably led to a silent war between locals and newcomers. The police couldn't cope. The mansions of wealthy families were ransacked, as were the communal dormitories. Those who spent the night exposed to the elements had nothing but the blankets given them by the government; nothing to lose but their lives. Some locals formed groups and sought to kill them to avoid the pestilence spreading. Finally, the Mayor decided the sick people should be taken to the other side of the Mondego River and the iron bridge closed off as a precaution.

Seeing what was taking place in the streets, the tramp sheltered Alma in his basement. For the first four months, the fever didn't yield. There were rare moments when Alma showed signs of life. Then she would fall back into sleep, open-mouthed, her eyes vacant, or she would become delirious, once again abandoning the real world for the one of her dreams.

In her bed In his bed
in the basement in the tower
in Coimbra in the Castle
Alma dreamt Broyz dreamt
of Broyz, of Alma,
struck by fever. struck by fever.

Yet their dreams were different, just as their feelings were not reciprocated, because Broyz knew he loved Alma, whereas she, by contrast, was not so sure. If she had yielded to Broyz's desires, it wasn't because she loved him, but because she couldn't find any reasons or sufficient energy to refuse the refined seduction technique he had spun around her. Until Broyz appeared, no man had treated her with such impeccable manners, no longer as a servant, but as a woman. Alma couldn't deny she had considered the advantages of being pregnant and being protected by Broyz.

"Did I talk in my sleep? What did I say?" she asked when she awoke, afraid she may have uttered Broyz's name in her delirium.

However, something more complex had taken place in her

dreams. Just as Broyz's smiling face appeared in the midst of her fever, so Alma also thought she heard a loud voice in the distance saying, "Tomás, Tomás," and that same loud voice, at other times, addressed itself directly to her, or to Broyz's jovial face, repeating the name Tomás. Whether it was pure imagination or whether someone had indeed uttered those words, she couldn't help shivering every time she heard that name, "Tomás, Tomás." Nothing like that had ever happened with any other name. When, from the remote corner of her dream those voices repeating "Tomás, Tomás" reached her, she reacted in an alarmed fashion, as though her own name was really Tomás and not Alma.

She also thought a man, who looked like the tramp, although older, visited the basement. Perhaps that man's voice calling "Tomás, Tomás" had encroached on her dreams. However, she saw so poorly through the veil of her fever that, at other times, that man was the tramp himself, somewhat younger and better dressed, as if the beard and shabby clothes constituted part of a disguise he could take on and off.

Soon, in her dreams, the figure of Broyz began to be confused with that of the tramp, without her being able to do anything about it. Yet the one Alma dreamt about was not the tramp she was accustomed to, but another one, who looked impeccable, a smart tramp, shaved and well-dressed. He wasn't just a figment of her imagination either, but what she did indeed see on surfacing from her nightmares. For when Alma opened her eyes, there he was, looking at her in silence.

The fever abated halfway through the sixth month of her pregnancy. The epidemic in Coimbra seemed under control and Tomás felt Alma was in better spirits. She even took her meals three times a day. She no longer moaned in her sleep. Her skin, whiter before than the sheets, was regaining some colour and her belly was now that of a pregnant woman.

One morning, Alma woke earlier than usual to discover Tomás writing in printed letters what looked to be a pamphlet. Realizing he had been caught, Tomás raised his hands. Yes, it was him who drafted those proclamations against Doctor Broyz. Nobody paid him, and he did it out of spite, to take his revenge on several men, he said, and that person called Broyz summed up all of them.

Alma wanted to get up and leave, or get up and slap him, or else get up and order him to go and leave her alone for a while, but she was too weak for such alternatives. She barely managed two unsteady steps before falling into Tomás' arms.

"What's the matter?" he asked.

He didn't understand this untimely reaction, just as he was completely unaware of what bound her to Broyz and the castle, what, in effect, bound her to the object of his revenge.

He walked her back to bed and gave her a sedative. Nonetheless, Alma was still indignant when she awoke.

"What are these pamphlets for? What's the point of defaming Doctor Broyz?" she said, trying again to rise from the bed.

On more than one occasion since her recovery, Alma had attempted to leave the basement. This time, however, she seemed absolutely determined to leave, although, in order to do so, she would have to drag herself out.

"What?" asked Tomás. "Are you leaving? Are you capable of doing that to me? Don't go, Alma. I've something to tell you."

And so he told her his name was Tomás Filho, although in actual fact his real name was Tomás Antunes Coelho. "I swear it, but I cannot prove it." He said he was heir to a castle situated near Vila Natal. "My father is Senhor Antunes Coelho, and my mother a servant at the Castle." Antunes had never recognized him as his son. "As soon as I was born, he sent me here, to Coimbra, to stay with an old friend of my mother." He said the friend, María Vitoria, brought him up as though her own, while not concealing the existence of Antunes and his real mother.

"My mother," said Tomás, "stayed on at the castle, obeying the senhor's wishes. One day I asked María Vitoria why my mother didn't escape. "Perhaps she has other children," she hazarded, but without conviction. In spite of all this, my mother found a way to write to us every now and then. At the beginning, she wrote to María Vitoria, imploring her to look after me well. When I became a man, she started to send me long personal letters. She told me about her life at the castle, but without details, for fear, I suppose, somebody would confiscate and read the letters. As well, into the bargain, my mother wrote very badly, not only with spelling mistakes, but also conjugated verbs unfortunately. From what I can understand, a servant helped her with the words, but he was of little use for many paragraphs were unintelligible and I had to decipher what she had meant to say."

Tomás said that once in a while his father sent him money. "My mother was unaware of it, and I couldn't tell her because I'd been forbidden to reply, in case someone found out about the letters she sent." According to María Vitoria, he said, by sending that money, Antunes managed to keep him away from the castle, to keep him living in Coimbra. "We were in no position to reject his money." Thanks to the money, he added, he'd led a privileged life until María Vitoria's death.

Inevitably, Tomás' feelings towards Antunes were hardly the best. He had periods when he hated him and flew into a rage: "Antunes isn't my father. Jesus Christ slept with my mother. I'm the Son of God." Then the money arrived, his fury subsided and he would talk of "my father". And then again he would recall his mother confined in the castle and would curse him again, as if they weren't of the same blood.

"When María Vitoria eventually died," said Tomás, "I concluded that if others became orphaned after losing their mother and father, I was the orphan of two mothers."

Tomás said it had been a lengthy process of abandonment. "First, my mother's letters stopped arriving, then the money Antunes used to send, and finally, María Vitoria died." Tomás said the day after María Vitoria's burial, someone banged on his door with his fists.

"I thought a creditor had come to reclaim the house. I thought I would end up living rough, like a tramp."

"Is anyone there?" he heard. "I've come from afar, I'm looking for the boy brought up by a woman called María Vitoria."

Immediately it struck Tomás that the person must be Antunes and he rushed to see his father's face, a face of which he had no knowledge. "That is, I didn't know what features awaited me: a fat man, or a man with a moustache, nothing, and what do I find?" Tomás said there he was, trembling before a strange, chubby man, dressed in airman's clothes, presenting himself as Antunes Coelho's envoy.

"I'm Captain Acevedo," the man said, introducing himself, scrutinzing Tomás, perhaps searching for a trait that reminded him of Antunes.

"According to the airman," said Tomás, "my father had died after my mother. Now, he felt it his duty to pay me a visit on his behalf."

"That means you're not a true messenger," said Tomás. The man laughed. "In reality, I consider myself to be a messenger who interprets what Antunes would have wished."

Tomás said the man was extremely pleasant. "He used an extravagant vocabulary, always trying to win my friendship." He said that, as he succeeded, and he knew he was succeeding, his confidence grew and he became even friendlier.

"I must tell you something very important," said the airman, getting right to the point. And he began to talk about the inheritance and Antunes' will. He warned Filho that if he didn't take certain measures all the money would pass into the hands of the man called Broyz, who had recently married Antunes' widow.

"What measures can I take?" asked Tomás. "Indeed ...", the airman said, and pondered. "Why did my father, who sent me money every so often, forget me when he drafted his will?" said Tomás. "Indeed ...", muttered the airman again, "it was an unforgivable omission."

Tomás knew he was caught in a trap. "How could I prove I had Antunes blood?" He said he'd even thought about going to the castle to speak with Broyz, or with the widow herself.

"However, Acevedo dissuaded me from taking such measures," said Tomás. "A few weeks later, when the epidemic broke out, I decided to take my revenge. You know, some people's only weapon is revenge, especially those who've lost before the battle commences."

"What sort of revenge?" asked Alma.

"Any sort," Tomás replied. "Mine, for example, was targeted at Broyz. I wrote threatening letters merely to ruin his peace of mind. As I knew quite a bit about him from the captain, that Broyz had studied medicine for example, I struck upon the idea of discrediting him. I wrote pamphlets, and one afternoon I circulated a list of obscenities among the students that I signed with his name. I did the same on the streets of Coimbra. Don't judge me too harshly … You have to understand I feed myself on this revenge. If I lose the desire to slander Broyz, what ambition would I have, what would I devote myself to? María Vitoria dead, my mother and Antunes dead, nobody to help me. I couldn't pay off my debts and I lost the house belonging to María Vitoria. I moved to this basement. And now you're offended by me, Alma … me who's looked after you as if you were my wife."

"On that last point he's right," thought Alma, as Tomás, in a paternal tone, said, "Come on, sleep, you mustn't grow weak," and planted a kiss on her forehead, an old person's kiss, before covering her again with the blanket.

Alma fell asleep straightaway, curling into a ball, her knees towards her chest. Instead of sleeping, Tomás spent the night watching the various positions she adopted, which the folds of the sheets permitted him to study. Around dawn, he undressed and slid gently, but resolutely, between the sheets. It was easy, too easy, to possess her, and for that reason perhaps, he shook her vigorously back and forth, trying to persuade his conscience that the girl wasn't asleep, had already woken, and that he had taken her without any resistance on her part. Gradually, Alma's belly began to move from side to side. Kissing her, caressing her with no sense of hurry, Tomás came to appreciate the fullness of her beauty, the smoothness of her skin, a skin that smelt like a baby's. Only the increasingly violent and brusque movements of her belly distracted him. These weren't the "belly in" sort of movements he was more familiar with, but "belly out" movements, if such a term existed, and they were pushing him out more than drawing him in. Perhaps it was involuntary, he thought, for the hands clasped around the back of his neck in no way rejected him, but then Tomás had never possessed a pregnant woman. This time was different. It had to be different. Particularly as the woman was pregnant by another man. He wasn't overly concerned to know whom was the father. He felt his desire wane. It happened suddenly. It was that belly that was largely responsible, not him, not Alma, not even the creature trapped in the belly, but the belly itself: a thrust of something strange between the pair of them.

Now that Alma had recovered, Tomás left the basement more often. Where he went and how he obtained those large loaves of bread and chunks of cheese with which he frequently returned was something that intrigued her, given that, according to her calculations, the tramp had no money.

One afternoon when Tomás was out, Alma gathered her energies and, still incapable of standing, crawled on hands and knees to the box where she knew Tomás kept his pamphlets. As she edged across the floor, she contemplated with regret that Tomás should hate Broyz. Both were good men, perhaps the best she'd ever known. What a shame the dictates of a will should come between them.

What if she confessed to Tomás about her relationship with Broyz? It wasn't a bad idea. She could offer him a section of the castle or a few hectares of adjoining parkland as payment for his troubles and in return for leaving Broyz in peace. It was very likely Tomás would be offended by such an offer: a derogatory gift that would only interfere with his plan for the revenge that so impassioned him. The idea of a reward wasn't bad, Alma thought, before quickly chasing it away. What was going on in her head? How dare she take decisions, albeit imaginary ones, with respect to someone else's belongings? What would Broyz say if he saw her return with a stranger to whom he must grant lands and riches?

She reflected all this as she moved towards the box, opened it and found it empty. Evidently, Tomás had gone out to distribute pamphlets. Of course, it was Monday. At that moment he'd be stationed in the Rua Ruí Fernandes, within the embrace of the policeman's complicity. She felt the hatred return in her, the same as she had felt a few days earlier, yet at the same time she had to admit her feeling of hatred was unjustified. She couldn't accuse him of anything. Had Tomás actually promised to stop distributing pamphlets?

Suddenly she heard a key turn in the lock. "It's Tomás," she thought, alarmed. She managed to shut the box, but the door opened before she could drag herself back to bed. Paralyzed, unable to move, caught halfway between the box and the bed she realized with bewilderment that it wasn't Tomás shutting the door, but another man whom she was unable to identify from her position on the floor.

"Are you okay, little one?" asked the man, seeing her down there, on her knees.

"Yes, yes ..." she stammered.

"What happened? Are you looking for something? Can't you get up on your own?"

Alma appeared to have lost something and the man offered to help. He crouched down next to her and, breathing heavily, with his cheek practically touching the floor, looked beneath the mattress. Yes, there was some object there, close to the foot of the bed, something shiny, something like rubies or precious stones. He stretched his arm under the bed until his fingers brushed against the object.

"I have it," he said. He then turned to her and Alma had to stifle a cry. Captain Acevedo! Of course, now she understood: it was Acevedo's familiar face she'd thought she'd seen during her fever.

"Let's have a look, what've we got here?" said the airman, fitting his pair of golden spectacles. His placid expression immediately transformed into one of surprise.

"The bracelet from the castle!" he exclaimed, without recognizing Alma. There were so many servants and chambermaids around the Antunes family it was impossible to remember all the names and faces.

Alma waited impatiently for the airman to return the bracelet. However, Acevedo was so baffled at the discovery of this object that, having climbed to his feet, he abruptly departed, taking it with him.

"Hey ... captain!" Alma exclaimed, just as Acevedo was shutting the door, realizing too late that by uttering that word it showed she knew who he was. She called out again, immediately, this time saying, "senhor, senhor," instead of "captain," but the mistake had already been made.

Alma had been delirious for so long during the past months that, over the next few days, when the airman didn't reappear, she ascribed the memory of his visit to her fever. Nevertheless, she couldn't find the bracelet anywhere in the basement, and, on Friday afternoon, the unmistakable rumble of the aeroplane flying dangerously over the houses confirmed Acevodo's presence.

An indignant shout was heard in the street:

"Are you crazy, flying like that?"

Nonetheless, the rumble continued as the aeroplane flew over the walls and doorways of the old dwelling places.

Some hours later, just before midnight, Alma heard someone knocking at the basement door. Tomás went to open it quietly so as not to wake her. He greeted the visitor outside and shut the door carefully, but a small ceiling-high window, slightly ajar, was enough for Alma to recognize the other voice.

The conversation between Acevedo and Tomás, at first no more than a murmur, gradually became audible. From the bed, she caught isolated words (*will ... castle ... bracelet ... servant ... Broyz ... aeroplane ... epidemic ... Antunes Coelho ... Broyz ...*) and as none were without meaning for her, their combined effect sent shivers through her flesh.

The voices died and the door reopened. Tomás entered with something in his hand. It looked like a loaf of bread, a gift from the airman. Was that how Tomás obtained his provisions? He broke the bread in two. He ate one portion and placed the other on a plate that he left on the floor beside the bed.

The following morning, Alma noticed Tomás was behaving

resentfully towards her, and she attributed this sudden hostility to the captain's intervention. She determined to reveal her true identity to Tomás. Levering herself up by using her elbows and the heels of her feet, she called out, "Tomás, Tomás." He stood before the mirror, completely naked. He was shaving with his eyes closed, and he continued to do so, as though he hadn't heard her. It was always the same: when Tomás drew the razor across his face, half-closing his eyes, Alma could look at his calves and thighs without being seen, his neck and back too, indeed, all his vulnerability was laid bare. Yet, on this occasion, as she contemplated him, she felt a tremor of fear and wished he would open his eyes.

"I have to tell him about my past at the castle with Broyz," she thought. However, an untimely sense of shame inhibited her from talking about something so vital before a naked man, and so she postponed her confession until later, when he dressed. Yet whenever she looked across at him, he remained there before the mirror, naked, slowly shaving where there was no longer even the shadow of a beard.

How would Tomás react to such a confession? She let herself fall face down between the sheets, and pretended to be still asleep, although she peeked out every now and again to see if he had dressed. Eventually, she felt two hands on her shoulders, shaking her with some force.

"Why did you hide everything about the castle from me? The captain told me. I don't understand why you hid all that."

CHAPTER NINE

AGUA had not forgiven the captain whom, after leaving with Senhora Amaral, failed to return to the castle to fetch him. Unlike Broyz, who remained waiting for Alma; unlike Alves, who felt it his duty to stay and tend the sick in the village; unlike either, throughout that time Agua waited only for the aeroplane's return. Thus, when Acevedo finally reappeared at the castle, twenty weeks later, on Christmas Day 1923 to be exact, Luís Agua could scarcely contain his impulse to insult him.

Predicting they would demand explanations on landing, during the flight, Acevedo prepared a lengthy reply by way of excuse:

"That day I departed with Senhora Amaral, you remember, the engine spluttered just fifteen minutes into the flight. I tried to turn back, but the wind carried me away. We were worried because from the air we couldn't make out any open spaces to land, not until suddenly when we spotted a huge field. As we touched down one wing cracked against the ground, breaking in two, and Senhora Amaral, who was already quite weak, struck her head against a handle and lost consciousness. Four farmers came out of curiosity to inspect the aeroplane. Having helped to lift the senhora from the aeroplane, they said Coimbra wasn't far away, or, at least, not as far as I'd supposed. I obtained a cart and horse, and took the senhora with me so that a doctor in the city could attend to her, but there was nothing to be done in Coimbra for she had lost too much blood on the journey, and her condition was hopeless. Having arranged a Christian burial for her, I went in search of a mechanic. No, pardon, first I acquired a set of tools, and then realized I had no idea who those farmers were, or the precise location of the small farm where my aeroplane was … and afterwards, what happened? Ah, yes, yes, afterwards I lost several weeks wandering across the vast plain, house by house, trying to describe the four farmers, whose features I couldn't really recall. For a while, I imagined the horse would lead me back, like a messenger pigeon that returns to its point of departure, but the poor animal could barely remain on its feet for more than an hour before lying down on the ground, rejecting my exhortations and attempts to shift it. Finally, when I was on the edge of despair, I came across the farmers and they took me back to the aeroplane. I don't exactly remember after that … I suppose I checked it over … yes, I think that's what happened … I needed some help from a mechanic, for the repairs, and all that explains my totally involuntary delay."

Nothing in the story was actually a lie, though many details were lacking, for example, having arrived in Coimbra, the captain had wasted several days seeking Tomás Filho's new home, instead of pursuing the repairs for his aeroplane. Luís Agua was unaware of this, that's obvious, and had no alternative but to believe the captain. Yet, even though Acevedo had committed this excuse to memory, Agua noticed how he stumbled over his words in many places. Something during the course of the journey from Coimbra to the castle had distracted the airman, making it difficult to remember exactly, and that was, when he was approaching Vila Natal, the captain had seen two faint clouds after all those months of clear sky. In fact, it didn't matter how he manoeuvred the aeroplane, the clouds seemed to be attached to its tail.

"There, you see," he said, "we all came on the journey together, the aeroplane, clouds and me."

An ironic smile flashed across Luís Agua's face.

"The doctor would have liked to have seen those clouds, I'm sure. But it's too late."

Too late? Those two words startled the captain. He was eager to know what other events had taken place during his absence. Something told him there had been changes, and he longed for Agua to dispense with that distant and recriminatory attitude and fill him in on recent happenings.

Gradually, he managed to find out what had happened. Doctor Alves had fought right up till his last breath in Vila Natal, sacrificing himself like an admiral in a doomed shipwreck. The epidemic had drawn to an end, wiping out everyone in the process, except those who had fled in time. Neither the friar, nor his altar boys, nor the occupants of the house in Rua Simoes had survived.

As for Broyz, he was very ill, said Luís Agua, who, incredibly as it seemed, was in better health than when Acevedo left.

It struck the captain directly that Agua had been the only one there to accept the potion invented by Alves. If the concoction had probably saved Agua, why hadn't it done the same for its inventor? Of course, two organisms never respond identically to the same medicine, or the same illness, but Acevedo sought to explain Agua's good health by means of another hypothesis. One was that coming from a modern city Agua enjoyed better health. Another saw him as a magician or illusionist, in other words, a sorcerer. The airman knew about the invention of electricity and, unlike the villagers, he didn't consider it an act of magic to switch on lights without the help of fire. Also, he remembered Agua's other talents, such as bottling little ships. And so, even though the second hypothesis seemed absurd initially, it amused him more than the first.

"Would you like to see Broyz?" Agua asked, interrupting his reflections. "I warn you, there're risks of infection. But would you like to see him anyway?" he enquired again. As the airman agreed, he handed him an improvised mask he'd constructed.

"A magician, an inventor and a craftsman," thought the captain as he fitted the mask.

On their way to the battlement tower, Agua suddenly stopped before a low table where a rather discoloured notebook lay. The airman stopped too, realizing it was the doctor's notebook.

"Do you recognize it? When Alves announced he was leaving for the village, his one wish was for us to continue his diary of the sky until a cloud appeared. It seems, Acevedo, my friend, that today heralds the end of this notebook."

The airman was pleased Agua again treated him with a degree of affection. He was on the point of telling him, half-jokingly, half-seriously, that he had doubtlessly returned to the castle on a day filled with incidents, but the doctor's memory,

Broyz's convalescence and Agua's bitter welcome encouraged him to remain silent.

"Good Lord, Broyz is unrecognizable," he said, coming down from the top of the tower. "I don't think he'll see tomorrow."

"I thought the same, but he's been like that for days."

"Let's ship him aboard the aeroplane … take him to Coimbra to be cared for," said Acevedo, but Agua rejected the idea.

"That wouldn't save him, that'd make him suffer … he'd die on the way. He's critical, can't you see?"

Of course he could see. The man was dying, and he was totally powerless to help. What would have happened if the aeroplane had arrived a few days earlier? Though that idea tormented him, at the same time Broyz's imminent death drew a grin to his mouth that was … yes, a smile … a smile of relief, or worse still, the smile worn by those who've seen a plan, a wished-for objective, confirmed.

The captain controlled the grin as best he could. He ventured out into the park and took a long detour beyond the stables. He inspected the castle walls, saw how the crack in the tower had continued to grow, and calculated that in ten or fifteen years time that wing would be at risk of collapsing if nobody took the necessary precautions. Then, as night fell, he returned and asked Agua for a mattress and blanket. He had to sleep right away if he intended to depart the next day.

"Senhor Agua, I can take you too in the aeroplane, what do you say?"

"Can you take me to Lisbon? Has the blockade been lifted?"

The captain explained the blockade was still secure and his proposal was limited to a flight to Coimbra.

Agua frowned in a gesture of indecision.

"I don't know … it doesn't seem human to abandon Broyz."

"But Broyz is virtually dead! Whether you stay or not is of little consequence …" Acevedo insisted, unable to make the other reconsider.

"If Broyz died during the night, Agua would come with me,"

the airman thought. It wasn't impossible for such a thing to happen. After all, wasn't Broyz in his death throes? And while he considered this eventuality, realizing he was grinning once more, something surprising occurred. Agua pressed a two-way switch embedded in the wall and a beam of light bathed the flagstones in the hallway. Had he installed lights throughout the castle? Only partially, explained Agua. Shortly before his death, Dr Alves had returned from one of his trips to the village with a box from Lisbon, sent by the Douglas & Banks company. Inside was the extra generator Agua had asked for. There was also a brief note in which Senhor Pereira apologized for his earlier letter, annulling "the previously communicated sanction," given the company was "unaware of the epidemic," and inviting Agua to return to Lisbon "as soon as the blockade was lifted."

"Will that be your intention?" asked Acevedo. "Are you thinking of returning to Lisbon?"

"I suppose so," replied Agua, by which he meant there was nothing he wanted more, but the "suppose" he uttered, partly out of superstition and partly out of politeness, caused the captain a sudden moment of concern. What ulterior motives had made him install that light in the hallway? Why was he obstinately remaining there, rejecting his invitation to Coimbra? Was he genuinely concerned for Broyz's health or was he declining to leave because he coveted the castle? For one moment, he suspected the latter and wished fervently that a miracle might happen and Broyz pass away before dawn. He imagined Agua's face on waking to find Broyz lifeless. What new excuse would he invent to stay? He stood and went off to bed. At first light he climbed the spiral staircase and confirmed, disheartened, that Broyz was still breathing. He refuses to die, he reflected bitterly.

He climbed into his aeroplane and took off without saying goodbye to Agua. The nose of the aircraft pushed towards a completely overcast sky. Why is it always all or nothing? he asked. The clouds, for example. Where were those clouds when they were needed against the epidemic? Now, in one sky, he saw more clouds than in the whole of the last ten months.

Something along the same lines was happening with Agua who wanted to lay his hands on the castle. All or nothing? But that fortune belonged to Tomás Filho, and the moment had come for him to appear and reclaim it.

Back in Coimbra, he said nothing about Broyz's illness or the doctor's death in case Filho should waver, decide to delay his journey for longer and stick to his stubborn revenge.

"At one time, my boy, I counseled restraint and forbade you from going to the castle. Well, just as I restrained your impulse then, by the same token today, I'm ordering you to go. I've spoken with Senhor Broyz, and he's understood my reasons and awaits you."

The young man believed everything and asked what the next step should be.

"We leave tomorrow."

"Tomorrow? But that's not possible," Tomás apologized.

For a moment, the captain thought Filho was belittling his plans.

"I went to the castle just for you," he said without disguising his irritation. "What can be so important as to merit postponing the journey?"

Acevedo learnt that Alma's accouchement was imminent and Tomás had decided to remain in Coimbra until the child's arrival.

"It's a mistake, it's a mistake," the captain lamented, but he couldn't change Tomás' decision. Three days later, Filho was present at the birth of André, as though he were the boy's father.

They gave André all the necessary care and attention and, a week later, they left. Since the captain was prepared to make two flights, he took Alma and the child first, then intended returning to Coimbra to fetch Tomás. The castle appeared abandoned, deserted by its occupants. "Where's Agua?" asked Acevedo. "Where's Broyz?" wondered Alma, looking for him in silence. Her premonitions were not good.

As Acevedo prepared to take-off for Coimbra, Alma saw the figure of Agua outlined in the distance. She hurried towards him with André in her arms.

"Come, follow me, you're just in time," were Agua's first words as he led her towards the tower.

"Broyz? Are you taking me to Broyz?" asked Alma, who wanted to show André's face to his father.

If the agony he was enduring could be termed life, then Broyz was still alive in the tower.

"He's dying," Agua said.

On clambering up the tower, Alma stood in disbelief when she saw Broyz.

"Would you mind leaving us alone for a moment?"

Agua respected her wish. Without pausing to consider the risk of infection, Alma placed little André on his dying father's chest, in what became a fleeting counterpoint of two hearts.

"Broyz … Broyz …" she called, then whispered: "It's me." Broyz, however, was already in his death throes and heard no-one.

They stayed that way for a few minutes, until André began to cry and Alma realized only one heart was still beating and the counterpoint had been broken. She lifted André from Broyz's chest with utmost care, as though he wasn't dead, but asleep, as if the baby's absence might wake him. And then, for the first time since her return, Alma contemplated Broyz attentively. Even though the sunlight at that hour shone directly on the tower, only a few rays filtered through the curtains. In the semi-darkness and through the slight gap in the mouth of the dead body, she thought she noticed Broyz had lost his teeth, or at least the most visible front ones.

Then, as though a breeze had shaken the rigid body, the remaining tension in the muscles seeped away and the jaw opened wider, just enough for Alma to note his lack of teeth. Only when André stopped crying did she come to her senses and open the door, finding Agua staring at the floor gloomily, tears in his eyes. "That's it," she said, a lump in her throat, though she suspected Agua had been spying and already knew of Broyz's death.

Luís Agua handed her a handkerchief, led her back down the stairs and served her a glass of port, suggesting she relax on a sofa and recover from the journey and Broyz's death, so sudden for her, so long awaited for him. After all the time that had passed since the epidemic and her voyage to Coimbra, everything had become distorted: Agua now seemed in charge, welcoming her as the master of the place.

"What's going to happen with all this?" Alma wanted to ask, but she remained silent. "What will happen? Did Broyz leave a will?" Of course there was no will because Broyz never felt himself to be the owner of the castle.

The aeroplane returned a little later and Alma asked Acevedo and Tomás to help bury Broyz. Against the wishes of Alma and the captain, Agua maintained they should bury him in the Antunes' pantheon. Eventually, it was decided to bury him in the castle grounds, for in the cemetery there was still, said Acevedo, "serious risk of infection from the final traces of the epidemic".

That same evening, at the request of Agua and the captain, Tomás Filho began digging a pit in a remote corner of the park. He was digging the tomb of his rival, though no feeling of victory swelled his breast.

As evening fell the heavens opened. As it had been months since it last rained, the storm took six days to die, and the pit dug by Tomás was completely flooded. They had to dig another, this time less deep, to bury Broyz, although nobody bothered to fill in the first pit. It seemed a logical oversight, especially as the more important debate was beginning over the possession of the castle and lands.

"He wants to hold on to everything," said Acevedo to Alma.

"Who? Tomás?"

"No. I'm talking about Agua."

"I want to hold on to the castle," said Tomás to the captain.

"Of course, my boy."

"I have had no intention of holding on to the castle," said Luís Agua to Alma.

"That's not what Acevedo thinks."

"Acevedo believes we all think like him."

"You can stay on here," said Tomás to Agua.

"I suppose I should thank you, but this all stems from a misunderstanding … I cannot stay here … I must go to Lisbon."

And so they were engrossed in these conversations when three soldiers approached the castle, sullen faced, their weapons on their shoulders. In general, any military presence in Vila Natal was always the sign of bad news, but on this occasion the visit of the three soldiers was to notify them of the government's reassessment of the central zone and the end of the "plague frontier."

"Very well, Senhor Agua, now nothing prevents you from travelling to Lisbon. You've ten days to leave the Castle," stated Acevedo as soon as the soldiers departed.

Such an ultimatum was an unnecessary humiliation, and so Agua, in his turn, resolved to wait until the last minute of the ten stipulated days before showing any sign of movement. As the time drew closer, so the tension grew among them.

On the tenth day, Agua awoke at exactly two in the afternoon. The pulsating rumble of the aeroplane could be heard from the park. First he opened one eye, heard the shouts of the captain and Tomás, thought "they'll soon stop that," and then realized what it was about: they were shouting for him, calling his name. He didn't move from the bed. He felt hot and his forehead was beaded with a cold sweat that was totally alien to him. He remained put in bed for another fifteen minutes without moving, until Alma came to seek him out, telling him Acevedo was waiting, and the aeroplane was ready to depart. And so, then, only then, he understood the ultimatum was definite, they were throwing him out of the castle. He washed his face, peered at himself through the steamy mirror and stepped out into the park where the captain waited beside his aircraft.

Faced with the irremediable, Agua requested half an hour's grace and packed a bag with a few belongings. The aeroplane then imprinted itself on the sky and headed for Lisbon.

For a while, nothing happened, Agua and Acevedo kept their silence. Then the motor began to grumble, nothing serious, only troublesome noises, zac zac zap, mmm mmm, noises that usually served as an excuse for not making conversation during a trip, though in this case, on the contrary, the noises seemed to stimulate a conversation between the two travellers. At times, the mmm or the zap zac forced them to repeat a word. It was Acevedo who was the first to speak:

'Do you … mmm … realize, Agua, my friend, that castle could've … zac zac … been yours?"

"Mine?" Agua feigned surprise.

"If Alma had died, if I hadn't found Tomás, nobody would've … zap zac mmm mmm …"

"That's true," reflected Agua bitterly.

"If history had been otherwise," the captain continued: "if I still had power, I would've granted you a wing of the castle. Yet, I cannot … I decided to renounce power, and now I'm barely … mmm mmm … an airman."

Had Agua heard correctly, or had the zap zac and the mmm mmm distorted Acevedo's words? What did all that about "renouncing power" mean? The wind was swirling the words around and the zap zac were so penetrating that Agua couldn't think clearly.

CHAPTER TEN

THREE YEARS LATER, in August 1926, a woman paid a visit to Luís Agua at his home in Lisbon. "I'm the daughter of Mr Cross," she said. "Of whom?" he asked. "Cross … Roger Cross. Captain Acevedo told me where I could find you," she added, and Agua realized she was the daughter of Mister Roger.

The Englishman had died some time before and, in an act of goodwill Agua could not explain, bequeathed him a collection of miniature ships, as bizarre as it was useless. Still more extravagant was that the daughter should have travelled from London to fulfill her father's wishes. It soon became clear, however, that the woman's journey had other objectives, not related to ships, but to her husband, a ruddy-faced man who, donning his hat, introduced himself as, "Mr William D Cameron, Scottish businessman interested in exporting tea and spices to the Portuguese market".

Nobody ever imagined the Englishman might have a family in his country, still less a daughter. Luís Agua suspected she might have been an indiscretion, an adolescent mishap on the part of Mister Roger, given she was almost as old as Agua remembered the father to be, which meant she entered the world when the Englishman was still young.

The Englishman's grand-daughter, whose name was Angela, had also travelled with Mr William D Cameron and Mrs Cameron. She was a little less than thirty and had recently broken off her engagement to a banker from Manchester. At first, Agua considered her pretty, although phlegmatic. However, fairly quickly, that distance which Angela subjected him to, ended up charming him, and his problem then became one of how to approach the girl, how to overcome the obstacles she had set for him. The Cameron's return to London was drawing near and Agua had still not spoken to her alone.

Besides his job with the firm of Douglas & Banks, no longer as an itinerant representative but now in the works planning sector, Luís Agua also worked nights, from Thursday to Sunday, as a lighting and electricity technician in a Lisbon theatre owned by an old friend. It was partly a hobby, partly to earn extra money. At the theatre they were performing a modern version of a Shakespeare play. On Thursdays, unlike the weekends, there tended to be some empty seats, so Agua decided to offer three tickets to the Cameron family.

Since he was a friend of the owner, Agua received a free pass for two seats in the sixth row and another on its own a few rows further back. He also reserved a place for himself, next to the seat on its own, which he imagined Angela would occupy.

He spoke to his assistant and asked if he would replace him for the night. He explained how and when to switch on the lights, those in the auditorium during the interval, as well as those on stage during the performance. The director of the play had arranged a different lighting scheme for each act and this depended on switching various of the twenty lamps that crowned the stage. On a sheet Agua sketched a diagram of the positions of the twenty switches on the lighting table. He numbered the acts and marked the spotlights to be switched on in red ink and those to be switched off in black ink. The system was so straightforward the assistant couldn't go wrong.

Less simple, on the other hand, was the matter of stage-managing he and Angela to sit next to each other. What if Mr Cameron pre-empted his plan and sent his wife and daughter to row six while he took the seat reserved on its own? That was perfectly feasible. Yet, if Agua was cunning and good fortune played a hand, he and Angela would find themselves seated elbow to elbow well away from the Camerons.

Thursday arrived. Shortly before the curtain was raised, Agua looked out from an empty box and spotted the Camerons seated just as he wished: the parents in front, Angela in row thirteen. However, at that very moment, something unexpected happened when a fat man, confused as to his place, was accidentally taking the seat to Angela's left. "Damn," he muttered. That fat man had complicated his plans. Five or ten minutes into the performance, Agua intended to descend and casually take up the seat next to Angela, but now he foresaw himself having to argue with that fat man, pleading for his seat.

When the house lights dimmed and the actors appeared on stage, Agua slipped away and discreetly made his way to row fourteen, just behind the fat man. "You're in my seat," he whispered into his left ear. If he chose this ear and not the right one, it was because Angela sat to the right of the fat man, and Agua was trying to accomplish his manoeuvering unnoticed. It seemed the fat man's hearing in his left ear wasn't good. "What're you saying? ... what're you saying?" he exclaimed in annoyance, loud enough for some of the audience to admonish him. And then, just as Agua was trying to explain for a second time that he was sitting in his seat, the stage lights extinguished suddenly and the whole theatre was plunged in darkness. With uncalled for professionalism, the actors continued with their speeches, confusing the audience further. Was this blackout perhaps intentional? Was the director trying to suggest a meaning above and beyond the text?

Agua understood immediately that his assistant was having problems. After a few moments in darkness, a few lights began to come back on and the actors fell silent. They were not stage lights, but the auditorium lights. Angela noticed at that point that her companion in the seat to her left had changed. No longer the fat man, but Luís Agua. Such a sudden substitution seemed better to her than even the most practiced conjuring trick. She greeted Agua without fuss, as though she'd been waiting for him, and proceeded to comment about the previous scene, just as the lights switched off once more. Agua's assistant up there in the box was completely thrown: neither he, nor his boss, had foreseen that by not having an independent light on the switchboard the inevitable moment of darkness between the auditorium lights being switched off and the stage lights being switched on would be catastrophic for anyone not knowing the switch layout by heart.

At the second blackout Agua ran to the aid of his assistant. Before long the auditorium was restored to light and Angela discovered she'd been talking to herself for the previous two or three minutes, since Agua had vanished and not been replaced by the fat man, now sitting two rows back.

Behind the scenes the actor in the lead role was arguing heatedly with the director. "I've been distracted, I can't continue," he protested, while the director tried in vain to calm him.

The play eventually resumed. At the theatre director's request, Agua stayed in the box and the seat to Angela's left remained empty.

The lead actor, still in a bad mood, was declaiming, his head held aloft and his voice booming up into the Gods:

"*Will you encounter the house? My niece is desirous you should enter, if your trade be to her.*"

And the suitor:

"*I am bound to your niece, sir: I mean, she is the list of my voyage.*"

The suitor seemed not to have memorized his speech too well, every now and then looking to the prompter at his feet for help.

A dazzling set design that imitated the splendour of old castles surrounded the actors. And even though the ornaments made out of imitation gold and cardboard columns were no more than a cheap parody of any castle, Luís Agua couldn't help not feel a sudden wave of nostalgia each time the curtain was raised.

Shortly before the end of the performance, just as the company came back on stage to take their final round of applause, Agua received a visit in the lighting box from Angela, still amused by the trick of the seat and the lights.

"I came in search of you," she announced, resolutely.

"In search of me?"

"Come along, Senhor Magician, make me disappear from here, quick, so my parents don't notice anything," she said, laughing and covering her mouth with the palm of her hand.

One year and ten months later, Agua and Angela were married in Lisbon, the city where she resolved to settle despite pleas from the Camerons. They had two daughters and, even though they became wealthy, Agua never fulfilled his dream of purchasing the old castle that was still occupied by Alma and Tomás.

The marriage between Agua and Angela, however, had not taken place at once. Angela had first to travel to England to prepare for her final move to Portugal. During those months Agua spent waiting for word by post, he received two visits from Captain Acevedo. The first, without any apparent motive, seemed more an act of vigilance, an investigation on the airman's part. Was Luís Agua staying in Lisbon, or was he intending to return to the castle? In order to allay these suspicions, Agua told Acevedo of his imminent marriage and his new job in the theatre, and the captain went away satisfied, almost relieved to have heard the news.

The second visit was less brief and more cheerful. This time Acevedo couldn't wait to let him know that the following morning he would attempt a monumental feat, something never achieved by any pilot.

"If I achieve it, I'll go down in history as a pioneer. Having said that, my friend, you should know the most likely eventuality is failure, and in this case failure is tantamount to dying. It's best we should treat this meeting as a farewell. If I live to tell the tale, we shall meet again … but glory always seems unlikely."

"I don't understand …" said Agua, "you believe you're going to fail, yet you'll attempt it all the same?"

The captain shook his head and sighed, as if lamenting that Agua was unable to comprehend.

"Promise me something," said Acevedo. "If in one week you've not heard from me, go to the castle and hand this letter to Tomás and Alma."

Agua said that yes, he would go, while at the same time trying to determine why Acevedo was saying goodbye to him in person and only by letter to the young people for whom, without doubt, he felt a greater affection. Perhaps that was why he wasn't visiting them, he reasoned, to avoid a distressing farewell. Or maybe he was afraid Alma and Tomás might dissuade him from his "exploit."

Luís Agua spent a week waiting equally for news from Angela and from Acevedo. On the 19th of May, a few days after the agreed date, and seeing as there was no news about the "exploit" that Acevedo had not specified, he set off for the castle armed with the letter.

On arrival on the evening of Friday the 20th, Agua had the impression things had changed, as though the images that had remained with him from the days of the epidemic were somehow all mistaken. The crack that ran across the base of the tower was in a desperate condition. The sense of luxury and splendour was not as grand as he remembered, in fact, the cheap décor in the Lisbon theatre now seemed more noble than the old furnishings in the castle. In short, a spell had been broken, and Agua sensed that sudden disenchantment we have when the light of day is cast upon objects that for the night we imagined to be magnificent. His experience in the theatre helped him to understand this situation: if distance was enough to transform the lamentable props on the stage into something lavish, was not a reverse phenomenon taking place on this visit, a substantial change in his point of view making him perceive as false and lifeless objects that were splendid before?

Tomás welcomed him with open arms. He was asking what had brought him back, a frank question, without the sneaking suspicions of the aviator, when Alma appeared, altogether a changed person. She no longer seemed the shy young girl who once served her masters, instead she walked with her head high, with such a petulance that it complemented Filho's *nouveau-riche* look. Seeing the transformation that ownership of the castle had wrought in them, Luís Agua regretted his return. He didn't want to lose the good memories and considered spending the night in Vila Natal not the castle. But the old village no longer existed. After the epidemic it was christened "the village of death" in Coimbra, and the elements and neglect had taken their toll on the old houses.

Unaware of what had become of the captain and his mysterious "exploits," Agua recounted his last meeting with Acevedo. He was very much afraid, he said, that by this time he would be dead. Then he handed Tomás the letter, which he read aloud.

Lisbon, Monday 2nd May, 1927

Dear Filho,

I will fly higher than ever, higher than I've ever done. I'll touch the sun with the tip of my left wing and from the vaults of the earth I'll fall into the sea and let the waters embrace me.

Before the final embrace, I write this letter to hug you, my boy. I no longer have any reasons to hide my true story.

Tomás, it is I. The one who writes to you, it's me, your father. The one who writes on this day, the 2nd of May, on the eve of his death, is not Captain Acevedo. The captain no longer exists, he died years ago and what has been spared by the worms lies in the sacred ground in Vila Natal beneath a tombstone bearing a different name. That's how it is, Tomás. I know, you'll think old Acevedo has gone slightly mad. That's nothing new. I know, you'll interpret my suicidal exploits as an act that confirms my madness. I only ask, my boy, that you read this letter before jumping to conclusions.

I take two thousand questions with me to the sea. The first: what does it mean, Tomás, 'to be marked'? For sure, it doesn't need much thought. For instance, your life in Coimbra wasn't it marked by your impossibility to go and live in the castle with your mother? Then, didn't you wish to be born in another place, in another time, to another father? I bet you did. Can't you imagine therefore something similar happening in my case? I know, I know, you'll say, 'but Antunes was born in a castle, in the bosom of a wealthy family, that's not being marked, that's something else'. I can hear you, my boy, that's what you're thinking at this moment. All the same, let's suppose a rich man can also feel himself marked.

In my case I knew I was marked on the last day of 1899. Midnight approached, farewell old century, we prepared to raise our glasses ... it's no mean thing welcoming a new century, I mean it's not something one celebrates every day, there're men and women who're born and die within the same century having never seen its beginning or end ... and so, Tomás, everyone was raising their glasses and counting, my boy, that backwards count that takes place every New Year's Eve, ten, nine, eight ... when a thought struck me ... four, three, two ... a gloomy thought I'd rejected until that point ... one, happy new century, everyone shouted, and I was brooding, thinking: "I'm going to live here forever, I'm going to die here, in this old castle". The

149

massive wall of stone would paralyse my dreams. The centuries were passing but the pile still remained there, solid and unshakeable. You can imagine my anguish, Tomás, because nobody wants to know how his life will be in advance. Yet, that night, I was hostage to all the Antunes of the past, all making toasts around me. The family had amassed its fortune and now I had to look after it. That, my boy, was that my destiny? To stay forever in the castle, a solitary miser seated atop a mountain of gold.

How could I free myself? I wanted to be an astronomer, travel the world, voyage in a balloon, have a thousand women, and write my life on white paper. Ah, but the family wouldn't let me go. And don't forget the castle either, because, though inanimate, it too manages to bind and gag. Once upon a time, my boy, huge castles were the symbol of adventure. They weren't refuges for the sedentary lives of noble families, distant conquests were witnessed from those towers ... everything that lay between one castle and the next was territory to discover. They were built as places from which to venture forth ... but those days have long since gone, and I wasn't prepared to serve as a keeper for a mausoleum in ruins.

I was still young and the century was new when, in an atheistic book that I obtained without the knowledge of my family, I discovered a sentence not necessarily true, but incisive and powerful: 'Freedom is the possibility to realize an irreversible act'. For years this sentence remained as a consolation in the reservoirs of my memory. One day I thought to refute it. In spite of the unlimited and arbitrary power that the name Antunes conferred on me, and even though I was capable of realizing any number of irreversible acts that affected the castle, the servants, or even the village, I wasn't gaining freedom by doing so. It so happened, Tomás, that all these irremediable acts I could potentially bring about didn't have any affect on my life, or hardly any, that's to say they were irreversible only for others. However, I needed an act that would be irremediable to me, and that by its very nature, would free me, beyond the castle to a place in which other irremediable acts were also possible.

How could I free myself? It was that same thing that alienated me from my parents that also made my freedom possible. My father was dead, my mother in the throes of death, and in a few months I would be the only Antunes Coelho alive. All that tied me was the castle and my marriage to Fernanda, of course. When I realized nobody else shared my blood, I felt something no other Antunes had ever felt: the certainty that I wouldn't leave a descendant in this miserable world. One day I looked at myself in the mirror, and what did I see? Captain Acevedo, the real captain, laughing in my face. I'd suspected as much for a long while … how shall I say it, my boy. I suspected that he and Fernanda had an understanding. I'm not saying she would have cheated on me, I don't believe that, she was far too upright and strict with herself, and, what was more, Acevedo was a loyal friend. Yet, they liked each other … when it comes down to it, Tomás, a man can smell it, just as when I arrived in Coimbra and met you with Alma, I smelt you liked each other. So it was enough to see the looks exchanged between Fernanda and Acevedo.

One sleepless night I hatched a plan. By handing over the castle and my wife to the captain, I'd be free. I would share the money with him. My ancestors had made such a fortune … your ancestors, my boy, that I'd have the means to live for years.

I remember when I proposed the plan. 'But, people, what will they say?' he said. 'To hell with people. People know my titles from memory, but they barely remember my face. They won't realize,' I replied.

'But, what about Friar Teresino? What will the Church say, will it recognize me as the new master?' he asked.

'To hell with Friar Teresino. I'll talk to him, and if necessary we'll make the greatest donation in church memory, and later there'll be a secret baptism,' I retorted.

'But, what about the servants?'

'Bah,' I answered. I was fed up with the trivialities preoccupying him. Why didn't he ask what Fernanda would say? He didn't ask because he already knew, he'd already spoken with her … of course they were in agreement … My boy, how happy it made me to confirm it … and the carefreeness of no longer being an Antunes, living like a dandy and travelling …

When Acevedo said he needed to consider my proposal, I decided to take advantage of the privileges of being master for the last time.

'Very well,' I said, 'I'll give you five days, but if the reply is negative, I'll kick you out without a centavo *in your pockets.'*

Good twist, eh, Tomás? How free I felt when Acevedo said yes. He too was smiling happily because by becoming Antunes, he was freeing himself just as much or more than I was, and, what's more, he was freeing his family after centuries of service at the castle. Therefore, that same position which had stifled my freedom would grant him his freedom.

As far as Fernanda was concerned, I suppose she took the Acevedo-Antunes agreement as an extension of the current state of affairs. Her future husband was not a stranger, but someone she knew well who would carry out my daily routines using my name. Rather than seeing it as a prolongation, she probably saw it as a revival. I'd been absent from her for so long, with a certain tendency to leave her be, as it were, that the new Antunes would revive the image of a husband. It was for these reasons that I knew Fernanda was happy.

And so, one day, with not much time before the substitution and my departure, a servant told me in tears that she was expecting my child. This meant I could be a father, I said. Fernanda was the one unable to conceive. Your mother, Tomás, was very beautiful … a woman of around twenty years, with your eyes and Alma's smile … farewell liberty, I told myself. Just when I had no ties … But as I'd already spoken to Friar Teresino, and we'd fixed a date for the baptism, it would have been an absurdity to dismantle everything just for a servant.

I met immediately with the captain and the notary of Vila Natal, with whom we'd previously drawn up the agreement for the exchange of roles. Maintaining my calm, I presented them with the problem. What should we do about this child on the way? 'Senhor Antunes handed me all his riches, but who can assure me that this child of his, when grown up, won't come to me with demands to reclaim his share,' asked the captain. Instead of talking to me directly, like a coward he addressed himself to the notary, as though I weren't there. 'If I were you,' the notary directed at me, 'once the child is born, I'd send him far away from the castle and his mother. It wouldn't be the first case of an illegitimate child that didn't know of his lineage or rights.' They convinced me, Tomás, and I spoke with Fabio that same day, giving orders for the young chamber-maid to be locked away in the stable, and, as soon as you were born, they were to send you to Coimbra, to Maria Vitoria's house.

I knew Maria Vitoria very well. Before moving to Coimbra, she'd worked in the castle, and during that time she and your mother had become good friends.

The day before my departure, at the last moment, I changed my plans and decided suddenly to stay until your birth. It seems inexplicable, I know. Nevertheless, a strange premonition held me back, a premonition confirmed when your mother, Tomás, died giving birth to you. Only then did I announce my departure. Friar Teresino gave his blessing to the newly-weds.

The captain, now master of the castle, made Fernanda a gift of the bracelet that Alma now wears, and I left without any further claims to the castle, carrying you in my arms to Maria Vitoria's house before venturing on my travels. I found the old servant, gave her a good sum of money and asked her to look after and educate you. I didn't tell her anything about your mother's death because I'd already instructed Fabio to write to you in Coimbra every now and again, passing himself off as her.

Of course, by giving him orders to write you, I betrayed the notary and Acevedo, but I knew very well that Fernanda couldn't be a mother and that sooner or later both she and the captain would leave this world behind. When that moment arrived, I knew the castle would be yours.

At that point, I felt truly free. Free, free. How I remember with such nostalgia those years when the future seemed endless. I made my own life, I travelled throughout Europe, by land and air, every now and then receiving news from Vila Natal, always good news. Until, one day, my substitute injured himself in a fencing practice. At first, the wound didn't seem too serious, then an unforeseen infection was declared, and one thing led to another, fever, gangrene, convulsions … and the death of Acevedo become Antunes.

The news reached me in Madrid. I had promised myself never to return to the castle, but learning of his death, I thought straightaway of Fernanda and the difficult moments she would be going through. I climbed into the aeroplane and headed there. To my surprise, of all the former servants, only old Fabio remained. The others welcomed me as though I were a perfect stranger.

From that day on my visits became frequent. An immense tenderness bound me to Fernanda. It wasn't love, but I felt impelled to care for her. During one of those visits she spoke about the will. Before his death, Acevedo-Antunes had added a strange clause: if Fernanda did not remarry, she could not inherit the Antunes Coelho family fortune. Stranger still, the man who should marry her would walk away with two-thirds of all the wealth.

'Does it surprise you?' said Fernanda, laughing. 'Good old Acevedo drew up this will in the hope we might remarry. Thus, the castle, money and titles would be reinstated to us.'

What I didn't know was if my substitute had plotted all this alone, on his deathbed, or if Fernanda had collaborated.

Weeks later when Fernanda suggested we remarry, I told her she was mad. She insisted. 'Let's do it for the money. After, we can each do as we please.' I said no, I wouldn't be trapped again.

That night I left for Paris where Resende expected me, and though I returned to Lisbon and Coimbra on several occasions to visit you, my boy, I only set foot in Vila Natal again a few years later when Mister Roger Cross, whom I'd kept in touch with by post, wrote to inform me about Fernanda's marriage to a certain Broyz. Damnation, I thought. This individual's arrival on the scene, Tomás, complicated your chances of inheriting the castle.

Tomás raised his face from the letter and looked at Alma, bewildered.

"This is incredible," he uttered.

Luís Agua tried to imagine what Tomás must be feeling at that moment, but his curiosity was greater than his compassion, and so he said:

"And the exploit? Keep reading, Tomás, please, let's see what the exploit was."

Tomás skipped two or three paragraphs he would read later, alone, and took up at the point where Acevedo spoke about the exploit:

Like a winged Christopher Columbus, tomorrow I will attempt to cross the Atlantic when I set off in the direction of New York. I know it's unlikely I'll succeed, but if I survive, my boy, I'll dedicate the heroic deed to you in the press.

You'll say I'm running away, and it's true, but I'm not doing so because of my terrible confession, I'm not escaping from the indignity of looking you in the eye … I'm running away, my boy, so that my battered adventurer's spirit will survive. I, who used to believe in progress as the new form of adventure, I, who used to whisper, 'the land can hardly support us, the sky is our challenge,' fear for a world that will become without epic, a restricted world. What, Tomás, are the brotherhood of man and the dawning of a modern era, if not mortal snares for the warrior spirit, for the old tradition of adventure? In a world bereft of adventure, nobody escapes anywhere. The only adventure left to me is this crossing of the Atlantic, and in that regard it's not so much an escape as a crossing from one shore to another.

I hope your life in the castle, by Alma's side, will be happy. Although I can imagine the pain this letter will cause you, I couldn't hide my true story from you forever, my boy.

It's probable I'll die somewhere in the ocean. If that happens, I trust that both of you, Alma and Tomás, will heed my last wish and adopt the name Antunes for you and your children.

A successful ocean crossing will proclaim the triumph of the spirit of scientific progress, in other words, the heroic feat; failure will proclaim the triumph of the warrior spirit, the deafening fall, in other words adventure.

Adventure is failure. No other escape than crashing into the sea.

With my wings, I hug you both.

The letter was signed: *A*.

After Tomás finished reading, such a heavy silence ensued that Agua couldn't tolerate it and went to the room Alma had prepared for him at the top of the battlement tower. He dreamt of Broyz, how could he not have done, and woke up with a start just at the moment in his dream when a crack caused the collapse of the tower.

He leapt from the bed and set out for a long walk in the park. The fields had been turned into modern lands for cultivation; pragmatic times. He took a closer look at the stable, now used as a storage area and garage for a red car, the latest model.

As he was leaving the stable, he stumbled over a mound of earth, fell forward a few metres, and was on the point of tumbling into a hole left dangerously open. He pulled himself together and shook the dust from his clothes, remembering it had been the original pit intended for Broyz's burial. Although the wind and rain had partially filled it, that hole was still there, looming large.

"A danger," he thought. Above all a danger for a young boy like André. By the time he returned from his walk, however, the incident was forgotten and, as he simply wanted to leave, he asked Tomás to drive him in his red car to the nearest station, where he could board the train for Lisbon. It was Sunday the 22nd of May. Stepping down from his compartment, he bought a copy of the *Diário de Notícias* and sat in a café near the Santa Apolonia station.

"AERONAUTICAL FEAT: MAN CROSSES THE ATLANTIC", proclaimed the headlines. Agua plunged in, searching for Acevedo's name: "The American, Charles Lindbergh, yesterday completed a solo crossing of the Atlantic Ocean, an unprecedented feat in the history of aviation," he read with disappointment. "Lindbergh set off last Friday from New York City and arrived today, Saturday, at Le Bourget airfield, France, where an excited crowd had gathered to welcome him."

AFTERWORD

According to Eduardo Berti, *Agua* began as a legal document, a will, one of a series of wills which he wrote in the late 1980s and which he attributed to various characters of his imagination. The will was that of a man who, at the end of the nineteenth century, left everything to his wife on condition that she marry again. Berti became intrigued by his own invention. Who was the man who had come up with such a peculiar requirement? How would the widow react under such constraining circumstances? What and where was this castle of which the only thing he knew was that it rose not far from an unwelcoming village?

In Kafka's novel, we never reach the castle whose invisible shadow falls over everything and everyone; in Berti's we hardly ever leave it. Its uncomfortable pomp holds together the seemingly infinite threads of the story, as character after character appears, performs his bits of business and either vanishes or becomes transformed into someone quite different, like the people in a dream. The castle on the outskirts of Vila Natal is a prison: for the widow Antunes Coelho, locked within its walls by her husband's will; for the young Broyz, who seems incapable of leaving in spite of the widow's pleas and the servants' opposition; for the village notables. who believe they will find a haven from the plague inside the ancient rooms; for the innocent Agua, who comes in search of quiet and finds himself entangled in a struggle between conservatism and progress, friends and enemies, truth and lies. The only escape seems to be death.

Berti seems completely unconcerned with assisting the reader by sticking to the story, because every true story (as Berti knows) grows in all directions, refuses to comply with the limits of the page. It may begin with the honest intention of telling how a travelling salesman in electrical installations, wishing for a simpler life, chooses a place which reminds him of a poem he once read. But this is merely the starting-point. Soon the story is not that of Agua but of the English art-expert, not that of the English art-expert, but that of the mysterious widow, not that of the widow but of her young suitor, not that of her suitor but that of the young maid willing to assist him, not that of the maid but that of an intrusive letter-writer, not that of the letter-writer but that of an aviator who alone can offer escape from the village bound by the plague.

Everything (or almost everything) in the story is a happy deceit: Agua, meaning "water" in Spanish, deals in fire, electrical fire; the village chosen by Agua is on no known map; the famous paintings sold at the castle are all fakes; the widow's hand, offered to Broyz Senior, is accepted by Broyz Junior; the cholera epidemic is really African fever; Alma, thought to be Broyz's deceiver, is in fact his true ally; *The Encyclopaedia of Buttocks* signed by Broyz is obviously not by Broyz; the widow's long-dead husband is not her husband; the man thought to be Thomas's father is not his father; Acevedo is not Acevedo. We are at the dawn of everything modern, of new beginnings and change. "*It was in 1915 that the old world came to an end,*" wrote D H Lawrence, quoted by Berti at the opening of *Agua*.

Berti's style is swift, almost breathless. He seems to be telling one thing when a disconcerting adjective, an unexpected verb suddenly veers the story off in another direction. He gives the impression of not being quite certain of what will prove important in the end, as if he (the author) did not know or had forgotten what the story was about, often giving us (the readers) the satisfying impression of understanding the plot better than he does. We guess that Agua is not going to find comfort in Vila Natal, we suspect that something darker underlies the widow's attitude, we can tell that Broyz is being manipulated by powerful enemies, and we wonder why the author does not see these subtleties as clearly as we do. In the hands of a lesser writer, such fragmentated complexities and hesitations would make us giddy or impatient. But Berti manages to keep us on track by providing us with detail after seemingly superfluous detail which, having caught our attention, then prove surprisingly essential to the whole. His masters in this are Adolfo Bioy

Casares and Witold Gombrowicz, two writers whose novels share with Berti's a distracted and unsettling tone.

Eduado Berti has published two other remarkable books: a collection of short stories, *Los pájaros* and one other novel, *La mujer de Wakefield*. But on the strength of *Agua* alone there is no doubt that he must be considered one of the most original, most accomplished novelists writing in Spanish today.

ALBERTO MANGUEL